ALPHA

ALPHA TIES

NORA ASH

Copyright © 2017 by Nora Ash

All rights reserved.

No part of this book may be reproduced in any form or by any electronic or mechanical means, including information storage and retrieval systems, without written permission from the author, except for the use of brief quotations in a book review.

This is a work of fiction. Any and all likeness to trademarks, corporations or persons, dead or alive, is purely coincidental.

ABOUT THE AUTHOR

Nora Ash writes thrilling romance and sexy paranormal fantasy.

Visit her website to learn more about her upcoming books.

WWW.NORA-ASH.COM

ONE

It usually takes a lot to shake me while I'm on the clock, but these political gatherings are tough to get through for most single women. I am no exception.

I grit my teeth and pretend like my system isn't being bombarded with alpha pheromones. As I glance to the side I can tell I'm not the only one in the throng of reporters who is on edge from all the airborn aggression—a couple of the other female journalists are fidgeting, and a burly man holding a video camera on his shoulders is flexing his free hand. Probably an alpha himself, judging by the size of him. But he's been through this before, as have we all, and we're all pretending like we're not noticing the testosterone rolling off the mayoral candidates in thick waves.

I clench my pen tighter and squirm in my chair from discomfort at the latent aggression as I take in the five candidates. Every single one is so obviously alpha, which I think is just another sound reason to avoid any and all politicians. When your job is not to cover them for the most volatile election in recent memory, of course.

"I'd like to offer you all my warmest welcome to this our third debate." The current Lord Mayor smiles from his podium up front, in what I'm sure his PR team meant to be a jovial manner. Lord Mayor Bremen is a man is his sixties, with dark gray hair and sharp eyes, and he has ruled Mattenburg with an iron fist for eight years. If there is one thing he's not, it's jovial.

"With only two weeks to election day, we have a busy schedule ahead of us, so let us get started with the evening's topic of CO_2 emissions and recreational planning."

I start to write notes on my trusty notepad, not bothering to look up while Bremen continues his introduction to the third subject the candidates have to discuss in a public forum before the elections.

"To get us started, I am certain Mister Peter Leod will enlighten us on the Liberals' viewpoints."

I look up, my pen pausing in time to see the Lord Mayor step backward and allow for one of the other candidates to take the floor. It is well known that he and Leod have been butting heads since before the election campaigns started, and as far as I know, Bremen has never allowed him to open a debate.

If Leod is as surprised by the gesture as I am—as the rest of the room appears to be—then he doesn't show it. He is a very tall man, who hides his alpha physique as best he can underneath an immaculately pressed, white shirt and a blue suit. No doubt in order to appeal to the liberal citizens his party represents—the ones who don't care for archaic roles and biologically dictated power structures. I probably would have voted for him myself, if it wasn't because I've been exposed to the lies and corruption within our city council for a few years now, thanks to my job. There are no Santa Claus, no Tooth Fairy and definitely no trustworthy politician in this city.

"Thank you, Lord Mayor." Leod lets his eyes sweep over the cameras and gathered reporters, the air of confidence that has made him rise from a relative nobody to a serious contender within the span of two years vibrating from him like a near-tangible entity.

I frown and stare at his defined features in the hopes of seeing even a glimmer of surprise or annoyance, but there is nothing but cool, calm self-assuredness. Maybe I'm just grasping at air, hoping to see something—*anything*—that will make a three-hour debate on CO_2 even slightly interesting.

I've barely had the thought when his sweeping gaze catches mine.

A jolt shoots through my body, almost like someone's sent an electric current through me. I blink, startled, and immediately proceed to drop my pen. I hurriedly close my knees and catch it in my skirt before it can clatter to the floor.

What the *hell* was that?

I clutch my pen tighter as I suppress the odd tingling

sensation in my tailbone left behind by whatever the hell that electric jolt was.

But when I look back up, *he* is still looking right at me, his cool, gray eyes seemingly boring into mine.

I am vaguely aware that my mouth hangs open and that tendrils of sensation are running down my arms until my fingertips buzz, but mainly, I'm just quietly freaking out. Why the hell is he *staring* at *me?* He looks… angry. His nostrils flare and a small frown makes its appearance on his forehead.

This makes no sense. I am certain he doesn't know me personally, and I've never written anything remotely exciting enough for a man like Leod to take notice.

It seems to dawn on him that he was meant to be talking right now, because he jerks his gaze away, smoothing the small frown as he resumes his speech.

I breathe a shaky sigh of relief at the loss of his attention, but I can't stop my hands from trembling. I don't understand what just happened—I don't understand why he was staring at me, and I certainly don't understand why my body is… is doing whatever the hell it is it's doing. The buzzing in my tailbone seems to intensify for every shuddered breath.

My bewildered thoughts come to an abrupt halt when my abdomen suddenly contracts in cramps. I manage to bite down on my yelp of surprise and pain, stifling it to a grunt.

The woman next to me gives me a puzzled look, but no one else seems to have noticed.

Sweat starts to trickle down my forehead, and my hands now shake worse than ever. Oh God, what is this? I frantically go through everything I've eaten all day to gage if it's a really poorly timed food poisoning, but I'm interrupted by another cramp low in my belly. I bite my tongue hard to avoid crying out, clutching my pen and now crumbled-up notepad as hard as I can until it's over.

I have to get out of here, before I barf on someone. Once it's finally over I scramble to my feet, doing my best not to make so much noise I draw any attention, and I manage to get to the passage that runs between the seated reporters before I have the next attack.

Only this time, it feels different. Instead of pain, an intense heat blooms in my abdomen. It's so strong I have to lean over and brace my hands against my knees while I gasp. And then, it's like something *snaps*. *Inside* of me.

I cry out as fluids rush from deep in my very core, and for a moment I think I am hemorrhaging. But the liquid that floods my panties and soaks through my skirt to make a puddle on the floor beneath me isn't red. It's clear.

I stare at it in uncomprehending shock for two full seconds, gasping for breath. What the *hell*?

A deep growl makes me look up, confused and embarrassed beyond belief. Everyone's staring at me, and apart from the unwavering growl, you can hear a pin drop.

I catch Leod's eyes as I desperately try to get a grasp on the situation, and freeze to the spot. His eyes are no longer cool gray but deep black, and his nostrils are flared. But he's not the one growling. Movement from closer by catches my attention in time to see the big alpha cameraman toss his equipment to the ground so it breaks into a thousand pieces.

I gape at him, briefly wondering what on earth he's doing, until I catch sight of his face. His nostrils are as flared as Leod's, and his eyes pure black. And he's coming for *me*.

The second he lunges, all hell breaks loose.

I scream, loud and shrilly as the giant of a man throws himself at me like a crazy person, but he's intercepted by another alpha. The newcomer grabs him by the shoulders and tosses him to the side, before he turns toward me. The same black look of insanity is in his eyes. The cameraman returns and swings a punch at his head, regaining his attention.

What the hell has gotten into them? I stumble backward, try to get away from them, but trip over someone's chair, lose my balance and fall on my ass with a squeal. Another hot, wet cramp deep in my abdomen makes me groan on impact and clutch my stomach.

"Get up!" someone hisses above me, and two small but surprisingly strong hands grab me underneath the armpits and pull me up. What I see when I'm once again vertical makes my jaw hit my chest.

The press conference has turned into a brawl. Fists are flying everywhere in the heaving throng of reporters and politicians, punctuated by loud growls and roars, and above it all is the unmistakable scent of alpha in rut. Of *multiple* alphas in rut.

"Dear God!" I whisper, clutching my bag like a safety blanket against my body. I've never seen anything like this. We are supposed to be civilized, supposed to have control over our baser instincts. But this... this is like being trapped in a cage with a pack of savage animals. "What the hell happened?!"

"*You* happened!" the voice from before hisses behind me. I spin around to blink at the person and find a redheaded woman with a 'Staff' badge on her blazer's lapel. "Come with me, *now*."

"I don't know what you mean," I protest, though I follow her as she grabs my arm and starts leading me through the fray of women and beta males trying to skirt the fighting alphas. Several have cameras pointed toward the middle of the brawl. She seems to know where she's going, and all I want right now is to get out of there so I can find somewhere to lay down until my cramps are over.

She shoots a pointed look over her shoulder at my crotch, where a wet patch is clearly visible. "You Presented. In the middle of twenty-plus alphas. What did you expect was gonna happen? Now let me get you the hell out of here, before any of those idiots get a hold of you and permanently wreck their careers."

I falter, shock numbing my muscles for a second, but the redhead continues to drag me along, taking us through an emergency exit door and pulling me into a deserted hallway. She pushes a key into the lock and twists it, securing the door.

"W-what do you mean, *Presented?*" I say, the note of

hysteria audible even to my own ears. "I would never...! I've *never...!*"

She draws in a deep breath and finally turns to look at me. "Look, just calm down. I'll get someone to take you home. You got a man waiting for you?"

"What? No. I live alone." I gape at her. "Why would you—"

The redhead lifts one shoulder at me in an almost apologetic gesture before she pulls out her walkie talkie. "I hope you've stocked up on batteries, then. Scott? I need a car to meet me at level 2. Make sure the driver is female, understood?" The last part she speaks into the walkie. "Some reporter chick freakin' Presented in the middle of Leod's speech. Damn press conference nearly turned into a live gang-bang."

TWO

"...multiple politicians were involved in the brawl that caused yesterday's press conference at the town hall to shut down, but experts say that none were as harmed by the incident as Peter Leod. As the face of the Liberal movement, his complete lack of restraint won't sit well with voters."

I cringe and bite back a humiliated whimper when my TV displays a clip of Leod jumping off the podium and into the fray of fighting men, his nostrils flared and his pupils blown—the poster image of an out of control alpha. Another clip, from a different angle, shows him facing off with Lord Mayor Bremen. Both men's expensive suits are ripped, displaying bulging muscles through the gashes.

"The incident happened when an unnamed female reporter Presented in the middle of the press conference. What triggered this biological response in the woman is unknown, but one thing's certain—we can expect to see

some major damage control from all parties in the upcoming weeks before the election."

I TURN off the TV when it cuts to Bremen, looking his stone cold psychopath self, attempting to "do damage control" by emphasizing his party's old stance on women in the work force. It's bad enough the most humiliating experience of my life has been broadcast on TV and distributed across the world via the wonders of YouTube—having the right wing use me as a launchpad for their outdated views is just adding salt to the wound.

A small twinge in my abdomen makes me grit my teeth in frustration. It's been twenty-four hours and *still* my body reminds me that is hasn't been taken care of like it needs.

Presenting. It's always been nothing more than an embarrassing topic in my high school biology lessons—something so deeply intimate an alien I, along with most other women I know, have never thought about it again after leaving high school behind. Why would I? I've always found nothing but disgust in how alphas use their biology to oppress others, and the knowledge that every single one of them is a domineering prick doesn't make the idea of being intimate with one any more appealing.

Not to mention their knots.

I shudder at the thought. I've never seen one myself, thankfully, but I've heard stories. Always whispered in hushed giggles among drunken girlfriends, never something anyone would dream of mentioning in polite company while sober. The thick, swelling gland on an alpha's genitals that locks his lover to him, whether she wants it or not, is always the butt of many crude jokes once the alcohol starts flowing, but also the horrific topic of more than a few rape survivor stories.

Unexpectedly, a shiver of desire travels up through my spine as the image of an alpha grabbing me by the hips and forcing me down over his huge knot, spreading me open far beyond what I've ever been before so he can claim me in the basest of ways flutters for my mind's eye.

"Fuck!" I curse in a futile attempt at giving air to the overwhelming sense of betrayal that follows that debauched urge. Isn't it bad enough I've spent most of last night fighting tooth and nail against my body's desperate need? That I freakin' *Presented* in front of all the city's reporters and politicians? Why is my biology *still* trying to undo the thin layer of civilization that separates us from devolving into wild beasts?

The next twinge from down low is interrupted by the sharp sound of my phone going off.

I suppress a groan and reach for it, cringing at the sight of the name on the display. My boss. My boss, who I haven't had the courage nor the inclination to get in touch with after I completely blew last night's deadline.

Praying silently that a miracle's struck and he's in a good mood I answer it.

"Yes?"

"You're suspended."

The immediate slap from the gruff voice on the other end makes me choke out a strangled cough. "But... no! Why?"

The second the question's past my lips I want to slap myself, but it's too late to take it back.

"I've been fending off irate calls from every fucking politician in this city, demanding your immediate termination if we ever want a single interview from any of them ever again." Despite the prickly tone, he sounds more exasperated than angry. Thank heaven for small favors, I guess.

"I..." I want to argue, but even as tears of frustration over the injustice of it all wells up in my eyes, I know it's useless. No editor in his right mind would risk his access to the town's politicians over a lowly reporter.

"Is it at least with pay?" I ask, doing my best to keep my voice calm.

He scoffs into the receiver. *"Not a chance, doll. Keep a low profile and I might let you have your job back once things have cooled down after the election."*

"Dammit Roy, this isn't fair," I hiss, losing my cool at the prospect of an entire month without any way of making ends meet. "It's not like I chose for it to happen! I... it's not my fault a group of over-wrought alphas can't keep it in their pants!"

This time, there's an amused tone to his snort. *"Always the idealist, huh? I'm afraid from their point of view, it's very much your fault they all lost their damn minds and nearly gang-banged a woman for open screen in the middle of prime-time, and you know how it goes. My hands are tied. Just count your blessings that none of them know your actual name, or things would look a lot worse for you. I'll be in touch after the election with an update on your continued employment."*

"Roy—" My protest is cut off by the call ending. I stare mutely at my phone, doing my best not to let the tears blinding me fall.

Fucking alphas! How will I eat? How will I pay my rent? It's not like I have a stack of cash in the bank to fall back on, not with how prices on everything from food to electricity have sky-rocketed these past few years. I pay nearly all my wages in rent as it is.

Why did this have to happen to me? Why? What on Earth caused my body to betray me like that?

All of a sudden I can't take it anymore. I need to get out of my small, dank apartment that still reeks of my humiliating desperation, and I need to get out now.

Irritated, I wipe at my eyes until my vision clears, before I throw on a sports bra and my jogging suit, shove my feet in my trainers and head out the door.

THREE

I take the back roads to the park, avoiding the throng of late-night shoppers and commuters. It's after nine PM, but in a city like this there are always people on the streets. Normally, I like being a city girl, but right now I'd give a lot to live in a remote hick town down South.

Of course, if I did, the entire town would likely know exactly who caused the embarrassing catastrophe at Town Hall last night.

Probably another lovely side-effect of Presenting.

I huff and jab my headphones in as I pass through the wrought iron gates into the dark park. Even in the relative silence, the sounds of the city around the patch of green still grate against my raw nerves. Probably another *lovely* side-effect of the hormones still lingering in my blood. Irritated, I turn up the volume and lose myself to the thrum of the bass.

That's probably why I don't notice them until it's much too late.

Fifteen minutes into my jog, a flash of light from behind a mass of bushes further down the path finally alerts me to the danger.

I pause, my steps faltering when the light abruptly disappears—as if someone shut it off to hide their presence.

Frowning, I fumble with my ear phones until the music fades into a low rush that mixes with the sounds of the city. Shuffling from where the light was seconds ago, like feet against grass, prickles at my ears.

"Hello?"

Hello. Not the brightest thing to call out into the dark. Flashes of statistics run through my mind as my heart rate picks up, headlines of violent crimes committed by the numerous gangs plaguing the city making me nauseous with fear. What am I doing here? No woman in her right mind goes out after dark, not to remote locations like this park!

But I was too lost in my own frustration, too hazed by the remnant hormones to think clearly.

"Hello yourself, *darling.*"

Every hair on my body stands on end at the mocking purr from further up ahead. Two large men step out from behind the bushes, one of them casually waving the knife in his right hand at me.

"Well, don't you just smell *delicious,*" the other says,

his lip pulling up in a mock-smile. "All ripe and ready for a fat knot."

Alphas.

I step backward, clenching my fists as I suppress a whimper. Now's not the time to start blubbering. Without giving them any time to preempt it, I spin around and run.

Loud whoops sound behind me.

"It's no use running, bitch!" one of them shouts. I keep running, as fast as I can. I've made it further into the park than I realized, and I mentally cuss myself for being so stupid. I *know* the damn statistics, I know what happens to a lot of women bold enough to go out on their own after dark. But call it deluded optimism or even just pure stupidity—I never thought it'd happen to *me*.

It won't, I silently promise myself, in between ragged gasps for breath as I sprint along the gravel path as fast as I can. I'll outrun them, I'll make it to the still populated streets—I won't become another statistic. *I won't, I won't, I won't!*

The crunch of gravel fifty yards further up the path makes my heart skip a beat, relief flooding through me. Someone's here, someone will help me—

The relief turns to icy dread in my veins when three large, dark shapes appear, blocking the path as they look at me. I stop cold, the fear in my gut reaching my throat.

Oh, God.

"Heeeere, pretty girly," one of the newcomers coos as he takes a menacing step forward. "I've got something real big to show ya!"

Footsteps from behind me make me spin around again, in time to see the two other alphas round the corner behind me in an unhurried jog. Both their faces are twisted with ugly smiles.

"Leave me alone!" It's meant to sound confident, but it comes out as a desperate squeak.

"Don't pretend like you're not gagging for a fuck." The bigger of the five grabs his crotch. "Give up your cunt willingly and we'll make sure it doesn't hurt. Much."

As terrified as I am and despite the wave of nausea that suggestion brings, some part of my brain is still functioning above the paralyzing fear threatening to take over. In their faces I see a complete lack of empathy and know they'll never listen to reason, and so I do the only thing I can. I keep running.

"Wrong choice, bitch!"

I don't turn my head to see who shouts the insult after me—I only focus on throwing myself through the thicket surrounding the path. The branches rip at my clothing and skin, drawing painful gashes in my flesh, but I don't slow down. If I do, I'm lost.

Only when I hear the unhurried sound of footfall and whoops from my left does my attention waver, and with a sick sense of dread I realize I'm being herded. They're *herding* me, like an animal, and I don't have time to figure out where to as I desperately crash through the undergrowth, heart pounding and the prayer of *'Please let me get out of this unscathed, please, please, please,'* running on repeat in my frantic mind.

Perhaps that's why I don't hear the rush of the river before it opens up in front of me, wide and deep.

I come to a halt at the very last moment, staggering on the edge of the slippery bank for a few seconds. When I regain my balance and spin around, the five alphas have formed a loose half-circle around me, about fifteen feet away. Blocking me in, with the cold river in my back.

"Told you not to run," the alpha farthest to the left purrs, the sound grating against my nerves. I've only ever heard alphas on TV make that noise, but this is such a cruel, mocking version of what's *supposed* to be the most comforting sound in the world it only makes every hair on my body stand on end.

"Please... don't hurt me."

It's the wrong thing to say—it's a stupid thing to say. We all know that they will hurt me, and take pleasure in doing so, but I can't stop the plea from bursting past my lips. Maybe somewhere, deep in one of them, there's a shred of humanity left close enough to the surface to hear me.

"Oh, *darling*," the man front and center, their leader, purrs mockingly, making another shudder of discomfort at the sound wracks my panic-frozen body. "If you didn't want it to hurt you shouldn't have run, now should you? You're gonna learn your place tonight and, baby, it's gonna *hurt*."

"Well, that and seeing how many cocks she can fit at once," a voice from the pack shouts, which is immediately accompanied by rough laughter. Tears of absolute terror obscure my vision, turning the pack of alphas into a menacing blur of heavy bodies.

"Time to open your legs, cunt."

This time, what bursts from my throat is a distressed cry, loud and shrill, and with it the numbness retreats from both my brain and my limbs.

"No! No, no, *no!*" I scream my denial out as they rush towards me, try to strike at them with my hands and feet, but they are too many and way, way too strong. I cry out again when a large hand impacts with my face, the slap momentarily dazing me with the pain shooting to the receptors in my brain, and then I'm face-down on the cold, muddy riverbank. Hands pin my arms down, hands press my face into the mud and a knee in the small of my back stops my wild attempts at fighting back as my clothes are ripped from my body.

Oh god, this is really happening. They will all take me, hurt me, use me, I think, praying despite all reason that they won't. That somehow they'll choose to stop.

My pulse is pounding in my throat and I can already taste the bile. This is not like being part of some statistics, not by a long shot. This is a living nightmare where I can taste, smell and—worst of all—*feel* every pull to my hair, every rip of my clothes against my skin as they tear at it in their savage urge to get to my unprotected body.

Their shouts become louder. At first I assume it's from the mounting excitement, like a pack of dogs yipping while they rip their prey apart, and I close my eyes in a feeble attempt at shielding at least a small part of myself from the brutality. But then the hands and bodies pressing me to the ground disappear.

The shouting, which my brain has muffled until it was only noise, as if to spare me the crude details of what will happen to me, slowly transforms back into distinguishable voices.

Anger. Fear. Pain. Some even sound as shrill as I did just moments ago.

Perplexed, I manage to roll to my back, but the sight that meets me makes me wish I hadn't.

The gang, or, the two who are left standing, have huddled together with their backs to each other, knives at the ready. Both are bleeding from long slashes to their arms, legs and torsos. The other three are ... I gulp and quickly look away from the savagely butchered bodies on the ground only a few feet away. Before I manage to avert my eyes from the gruesome display I recognize the cruel leader's cold eyes staring up at me from underneath a near bush.

His body is no longer attached to his head.

FOUR

A shadow moves in the darkness, and death follows in its wake. The faint light from the city reaching into the park gleams off cold steel as the newcomer finally makes himself known.

He whirls across the grass, and I hear the sick sound of metal slicing through flesh followed by wet gurgling. When the two remaining men fall to the ground, he finally stands still, staring down at the unmoving bodies. His victims.

He is a huge man, bulging muscles clear even in his shadowed outline. An alpha, no question about it.

It's not until he turns his attention to me that I notice the black mask covering the top half of his head.

No one with good intentions ever hides their face, and a new layer of goosebumps break out across my skin as I stare up at the silent alpha.

The silent killer.

Will he hurt me, too?

I don't dare take my eyes off the dark figure to glance at the slumped bodies I know litter the ground around us, but every hyper alert part of me knows they're there, the deadening silence enveloping us an imposing contrast to the fight just seconds ago.

He tilts his head, obviously looking at my still-sprawled form on the muddy ground, and my heart threatens to jump out of my throat.

"P-please. Don't kill me." It's a ridiculous plea, but I can't stop it from spilling past my lips even if someone who can kill with such ease as this alpha is unlikely to have an ounce of mercy in his body.

The alpha grunts, a sound of disgust or surprise I'm not sure, but when the steel dagger in his hand gleams against the faint city lights, it's because he wipes it on his pants before shoving it into its sheathe. A large hand extends toward me, hovering in the air above my face.

I stare mutely at the appendage. Is he... offering me a hand up?

The gesture seems so grotesquely out of place, considering the gore surrounding us, that I can't help the snort of amusement that breaks out of my fear-clenched throat. Horrified with myself, I slap a hand across my mouth, but he doesn't react to my faux pas. The hand still hovers above me, waiting for me to grasp it.

Well, if he wanted to kill me, he would have done so by now. Probably.

I move my hand from my mouth and carefully place it

in his, my fingertips brushing over soft leather as I do. He's wearing gloves.

Strong fingers close around my hand, and without preamble I am hoisted up off the ground to stand on my own, shaky feet. The alpha releases his hold on my hand the second I've regained my balance.

"T-thank you," I manage, not entirely sure if I mean for the hand up, or for saving me from the gang.

He saved me.

It's not until that moment it fully dawned on me that... that he killed those men to... save me?

"Did you... you killed them... for me?" I babble, my panic reaching new and unprecedented heights. "Oh God, am I an accomplice to murder? Shit, *fuck,* this day just cannot get any worse!"

It's not the sanest response to getting rescued from gang rape, some far-away part of me recognizes, but that part is somehow removed from the rest of me—who's busy having a complete break down. Pants around my ankles, top ripped and smeared in mud and the tone of hysteria clear in my increasingly high-pitched voice.

A large hand closes around my right shoulder, the strength in it evident from even the light squeeze that finally breaks through my hysteria.

"Calm yourself."

His voice is deep and gruff and one hundred percent *alpha.* It resonates down my spine and into my muscles, easing some of the tension in my body as only the authoritative command of an alpha can. I stare mutely up at him, not sure if I am thankful that he's stopped my spiraling breakdown or angry that a murderous stranger can have that sort of impact on my body. I shouldn't be any kind of *calm* right now, but my treacherous biology gives exactly zero fucks about what I think it *should* be doing.

"I'm sorry," I say when he releases his grip on me again, finally realizing that freaking out on the guy who just saved me from the ultimate pain and humiliation is neither polite nor particularly smart. Even if he did just kill five men in cold blood in front of me, and I still have no idea what he wants from me. If it's sex he's after, he could have taken it by now, and my life along with it.

I blame his alpha-influence over my nervous system for why I'm not more scared of him. Sure, my pulse is still drumming rapidly in my throat, but I'm not frightened for my life. I should be. I should be begging him for mercy or trying to run from him, however futile such an act would be.

"Um... I really appreciate it." I feel stupid even as I say it, partly because of the sentiment and partly because it finally dawns on me that my pants are still around my ankles. I want to bend to pick them up, but the urge to not take my eyes off him is stronger. Yeah, I might not be as scared as I ought to be, but even his influence can't completely numb out the rational voice in my brain screeching that I'm alone in an abandoned park with a masked killer. He's a predator, there's no question about it, and every instinct in my body's telling me that sudden movement is a very bad idea.

"I don't have any money on me, but—" My lips quiver when he takes a single step toward me.

"B-but if I can do anything to repay you, I will," I quickly stutter, the threat of his presence suddenly much sharper in the most primal part of my brain thanks to the too-close proximity of his huge body.

Yeah, he's an alpha all right. It's not just the sheer size of him—it's the powerful aura rolling off him in waves even as he keeps his body immobile in front of me. That unquestioning demand for submission. The completely unprovoked thought that he probably smells headier than any other male on the planet flashes through my mind, and I blink in shock at its unexpected passing.

"You think I am some vigilante saving damsels in distress in the hopes of a reward?"

His voice is surprisingly soft, though the alpha gruffness in it never wavers. It is velvet wrapped over an iron core, and it makes me shake, though I don't know why.

"No." There is nothing velvety about my own voice. It's as shaky as my body, hoarse from stress and screaming. It's the voice of prey, and I hope it doesn't trigger whatever violent instincts an alpha his size is bound to have in abundance. "I don't. But... who are you? I-if you don't mind me asking." I tag the last bit on when the idiocy of asking a masked killer for his identity hits me like a brick wall.

"I know who *you* are," he says, ignoring my question. I feel his eyes still shaded in the darkness trail up my body. The sensation makes me shiver despite the blood in my veins heating up. *Fucking alpha.* I never feel anything but mild fear and loathing for his kind—why is he different?

"You're the reporter who nearly caused a riot at Town Hall last night."

I gape up at him. "H-how do you know that?" Real smart admitting to that, but the surprise of his statement catches me off guard.

He cocks his head, the shape of his sensual mouth flattening into a line. "Who do you work for?"

"K-KTP News," I stutter, taken aback by the suddenly threatening undercurrent to his otherwise calming voice.

"I know your network," he sneers, and this time I'm sure I can detect anger. My ever-looming fear hikes up several notches in response. "What I don't know is who sent you to that press conference high as a kite on heat-hormones. Who's behind this? Who wants to discredit the Liberals bad enough to shove a foolish young girl on the cusp of Presenting into a roomful of alphas?"

Despite the insult of being called *'a foolish young girl'* at the age of twenty-six, I can't muster so much as a frown. For every word his voice gets sharper, and the alpha pheromones in the air turn from placating to aggressive. He's *pissed,* and it's wreaking havoc on my already frayed nerves.

"I.... I wasn't on any hormones. I-it just happened. I'm not trying to discredit anyone, I swear!"

"Bullshit," he hisses, and then he's right in front of me, the heat from his body radiating against mine. He grabs me by the back of my neck, cupping my head as he pulls me in while simultaneously dipping his face to my throat.

I whimper in confused panic, but the firm grip on my neck keeps me from trying to fight him off. I stand frozen, paralyzed like a kitten in its mother's grasp, and stare with huge eyes as he draws in a deep breath of my scent. His breath tickles across the skin of my throat, making every hair on my body stand on end, my nipples harden painfully against my ruined top.

"You still smell like desperation and sex." This time his voice is a low growl, the frustration still evident, but there's also a rich, sultry quality to it. "Like *heat*. Tempting any alpha you pass by. Do you *want* to get raped?"

There's something in his voice, that heated, sultry note, that suddenly makes it clear what his intended payment for my salvation might be. But instead of the outrage I *should* feel, something tense low in my abdomen melts in response. It's not until I realize I've gone lax in his grasp, letting him support my weight with his that it dawns on me what I'm doing. What I'm offering.

"No!" I jolt backward and away from him, the sheer shock at my own reaction to this stranger, this *killer*, jolting me out of whatever spell his presence is weaving over my confused mind. "Absolutely not!"

He lets me stumble out of his grip and a few steps away, and I nearly trip over my own pants.

Shaking like a leaf from how close I was to letting this stranger do what he wants with me, I bend to pick up my pants. I no longer care if I have to take my eyes off him to do so, I need to not be so exposed anymore.

My fingers are stiff from cold and shock, and the button and zipper are bust. Awkwardly, I cling on to them with one hand as I look back up at the alpha. I open my mouth to tell him thank you again for saving me, but I'm leaving now—but just then, our eyes finally meet and all that escapes my parted lips is a low grunt.

His eyes are a cool shade of gray—the eyes of a ruthless alpha for sure. But behind the facade there's something else. Something wild and deep and primal, and it's pulling on a part of me I never knew existed until this very moment.

Out of nowhere, a sharp twinge in my abdomen makes me whimper from surprise and pain, and I keel over, losing my grip on my pants as I rest my hands on my bare knees for the few seconds it takes before my body is released from the unexpected spasm. It is gone as swiftly as it came.

I blink, slowly straightening up.

No. No, no, no, not again! I stare at him, wide-eyed, the accusation of using some sort of biological warfare against me not completely formed in my mind when I'm hit by the next wave. This time, it's... different, and I recognize the heat blooming out from deep inside of me before arousal shakes through my body in fitful waves.

It can't be. Please, no.

The groan I involuntarily send into the air between us sounds like a pleading, *"Ooh"*.

Oh God, it's really happening again.

Slick moisture rushes from my core, flooding my pussy until a river of fluids gushes out and soaks my broken pants as my body presents for him, the alpha it mistakenly believes has been posturing for my favor.

Despite my body's mutiny, I feel my sense of civilization take a firm hold as the deepest blush of my lifetime spreads over my entire body. I slap the hand not clinging to my pants in front of my face with a humiliated whimper, curling in on myself while the pleasurable shocks preparing me for him—this killer—rake through me, stronger than anything I've felt before.

"Oh God!"

I whine through the expulsion of liquids and the opening of my channel in anticipation of his claiming, too mortified to look at the man who's done nothing to incite this response from my body.

It must be the adrenaline, the conquering of other alphas to save me, it must be... My thoughts are struggling to find reason during the onslaught of my most basic instincts, but finally I am released from the tremors, my body having completed the preparation. From my disastrous experience last night, I know my sex is flushed and opened, slick and ready for penetration, but all I sense is the soaked state of my thighs and clothes and the utter and complete humiliation of this horrific situation. Maybe, when I think back to this night later on, the worst parts will be the near-rape or the witnessing of a mass murder, but right now, those things are astonishingly hard to even remember.

He must think I am a lunatic. And he'd probably be right. I straighten slowly, forcing my hand from my face so I can apologize. I don't care who he is—there is no excuse for this vulgar display. None.

"I... I'm really sorry, I don't know why this keeps happening to me." My voice is a humiliated whisper.

He cocks his head at me, and I have to fight myself to not hide my face behind my hand again.

"I'm really sorry," I repeat, a frantic note making my voice shrill again. "This should never happen—it's so wrong, I'm so sorry." My fingers clutch at the fabric around my midriff, and I fumble desperately to secure them to preserve at least an echo of my dignity. I don't manage to make any headway before the air pressure shifts and I automatically glance up.

Once more, the alpha is right next to me, close enough to notice that his eyes now appear fully black, swallowed by dilated pupils. Without my conscious command my fingers release my pants, letting them slide back down.

Oh, God.

His nostrils flare, and a new rush of wetness drizzles down my thighs, as if my body's responding to his obvious scenting of me. Like I wasn't already drenched enough for even a normal person to smell my pheromones—they're so thick in the air I can practically taste them.

A wry smirk pulls on his full lips, and in that single

change of expression the ever-present predator leaps to the forefront.

"Oh, God!" I gasp as I see him removing the leather glove from one hand, carelessly letting it fall to the ground. My body clenches and shudders in primal recognition of what is written all over his face, even if my conscious mind still refuses to acknowledge it.

When his thick, warm finger reaches between my legs and dips into my slit I wish I'd saved the outburst for this. He pulls it up, dragging it through my folds all the way from my sopping hole to the aching nub burning at the top before lifting the digit slowly, provokingly, to his lips. I stare at him in shock when he opens his mouth to suck my fluids off.

His eyes flutter shut, a deep growl resonating from his throat and all the way into my spine sending a new gush down my thighs, and I whimper pathetically. Half from need, half from fear, because even before he says it I know there's only one way this can go now.

Black, primal demand flashes against me when his eyes open once more, the smirk still present—taunting.

He knows I won't be running this time.

FIVE

"I—I really don't think this is a good idea!"

Of all the things I could have said when faced with a rutting alpha, alone in a dark, abandoned park, that's probably not the best choice. Especially not since every cell in my body is thrumming with desperate need, and at the most primal level I know the only thing that'll cure me is him. Him, and everything his darkened eyes are promising he'll do to me.

He cocks his head at me again, and I get the distinct impression he's quirking an eyebrow at me underneath the mask. Not that I can blame him—despite the panic pulling sluggishly on my lust-soaked brain, I know he can scent my desperation for his touch. I might not know him, but my body knows he's the only one who can stop the aching deep inside of me.

But this is *wrong*. No respectable woman would yield

to a stranger like this, on a muddy river bank surrounded by corpses. *I can't do this—I can't, I can't, I can't.*

"Give me one good reason."

His low growl, deep and rich and so fucking *alpha* I can't help the whimper escaping my throat at the sound of it, makes me realize I've spoken out loud.

"I..." I fumble for an answer that will end this madness, that will let him release me so I can run home and hide until every last memory of this night has been wiped from my mind. But it's so hard to think when he's so close I can feel his heat penetrating through my skin and into my blood, and all I want is to give in to the unyielding demand I see in his lust-darkened eyes.

Not waiting for me to finish, he wraps an arm around my back as he slides his glove-less fingers down across my abdomen until he reaches my drenched sex. The lightest touch of his fingertips against my aching clit sends an explosion of white-hot sensation through my shaking body.

"I can see them!" I blurt out, pulling my upper body back from his even as my hips press forward in desperate pursuit for more. "I can't... we can't... I can see their blood and..."

A feral sneer pulls on his sensual mouth, and before I can blink he picks me up like I weigh nothing more than a rag doll and carries me through the maimed bodies on the ground to a nearby tree. Roughly, he puts me down and spins me around so I face the wide trunk.

"There," he growls behind me, his breath raising goosebumps along the back of my neck.

His hand presses against my spine until my shoulders meet the rough bark. When I twist my neck so my face is not against the surface I can no longer see the corpses.

Another hand roams down my back while I am pinned in place, following the curve of my ass until it reaches the soaking wetness between my legs where I am aching and clenching for this. But he is a stranger—I am panting and spread open for a killer, and I know I should fight him.

I want to flinch when his massive body moves to rest firmly against mine, but instead my hips push backwards and my legs part as wide as they can in the pants trapping my ankles. Everything I do seems an invitation to him, down to the small, impatient whines escaping my throat, and I can't stop myself, no matter what my muted reasoning is screaming from behind the thick veil of lust.

He bends his head over me, breathing deeply in the now shared air, and finally I am hit fully by his scent. He smells like ... like musk and *alpha* and raw sex. So much better, *fuller,* than anything and anyone I've ever scented in my life that there is hardly any comparison. My eyes roll back in their sockets as the last resistance leaves my strained mind.

He has accepted my offering. He will have me.

Large hands find my hips and I feel him shift behind me, lining up, and then firm heat presses against my soaking lips.

Yes, yes, yes!

The tension increases, but the relief of penetration doesn't follow. I arch my back further, desperate to accept his cock now that I have finally given in to nature's inescapable demand. I feel his flared head pressing against the soft, wet flesh so anxious to welcome him, and whimper with frustration. *Inside!* I need him *inside!*

"Please!" I pant, trying to back myself onto him, disregarding the pain I'm causing myself. He is so *thick*—if he will just fill me up like every instinct in my body is screaming for, I will be sated, I know it.

The hands on my hips catch my attempt at spearing myself on his cock, thumbs digging painfully into my skin when I buck against his restraint.

"I am your first alpha."

It is more of a statement than a question. I whine a confirmation nonetheless.

He growls angrily, causing my pussy to clench with pathetic need and a river of slick moisture to pour out of me and over his cock, but instead of pushing past my body's resistance and completing his claim he draws back, letting the cool night air brush over my exposed opening.

"No! What are you doing?" He can't leave me like this, unfulfilled and empty. I squirm, trying to twist around. I need him, I need—

Sharp teeth close around the back of my neck, sending shocks of pleasure straight to my nipples and clit. He growls again, warningly this time, and something in my brain clicks, freezing me in place.

He licks the nape of my neck, loosening his bite now that I have stilled again. I shudder at the sensation of his tongue, such a silky soft contrast to the hulking roughness of everything else about this alpha. It plays over every sensitive spot there, but the gentleness is soon shattered when his fingers slide from my hips and up under my ruined shirt and sports bra to pinch my nipples.

"*Ah!*" I cry out wordlessly, jerking from the unexpected pain, but he quickly bites back down on my neck again, triggering the same receptors as before, and I go lax, whimpering in confused surrender.

Another agonizing pinch follows, as if to assert his right to do with my body as he pleases, but this time I simply moan, locked in place by his jaws as I am.

Impatiently he smooths his gloveless hand down my stomach, and my hips, which have been firmly pressed back against his strong thighs until now, jerk forward in blind search of stimulation when he brushes over my bared mound.

Thankfully, he doesn't pause, but goes straight for my throbbing clit, circling it rapidly before dipping two fingers further down, coating them in my own lubrication. Then, he presses both firmly against my little nub, and my pants of, '*oh, oh, oh*' change to a shriek of pleasure. It burns through my blood, delicious and dark and perfect, but still... *wrong*. I am still empty of him, still not claimed, and no matter how good—oh god, *so fucking good*—it feels, I need more.

"Please... fuck me!" I manage to gasp out between

yowls as he attacks my sensitive clit. "Please, please, *please...!*"

The fingers leave, and I sob with frustrated need for three full seconds before both return to my exposed pussy, finding their ultimate goal. My entrance stretches eagerly when he thrusts his thick digits into me and I push my hips back against him once more, automatically assuming the position of a submitting female.

"*God!*" My voice is a hoarse whimper, my breath quick and labored. So close. This is *so close* to what I need. I thrust back against him, encouraging him to go deeper.

"Impatient girl." It sounds like a snarl against the back of my neck where he's still holding me in place, but quiet laughter brushes over my skin. He finds amusement in my plight.

I let out a sound I've never produced before: an angry yelp, like an animal in pain. This is not fucking funny!

A third finger presses into my clenching sheath and I groan, immediately distracted. He's stretching me deliciously, slowly pumping in and out, flexing his hand to spread me wider as he does.

"More, please!"

He releases my neck and obliges me, thrusting faster and as deep as he can. It's not deep enough—my cervix is weeping to be battered and conquered, and despite the wonderful pressure against my walls where he's spreading his fingers to widen me I feel anger at his incompetence flooding my brain now that my compliance isn't assured by his bite.

"What's *wrong* with you?" I snarl, forgetting myself—my place—in my desperate lust. *"Fuck* me! Are you not man enough? Take me!"

It's the wrong thing to say. Of course it's the wrong thing to say. He's an alpha, the most aggressive among males, but for my goal it is also the perfect incentive: the one thing that will make him give me what I need *right now.*

His fingers leave me and are on my hips before I can gasp. His furious growl resonates through the park while he aligns me with his cock, prepared to punish me for my words. Even an alpha as powerful as he cannot let a challenge to his virility stand, no matter how firmly his claim to the top of the food chain is already established.

The tip of his hard length touches me, deepening just enough to ensure that my flesh has adapted sufficiently from his hand's manipulation before his fingers dig painfully into my hips, assuring that I stay put.

And then he thrusts.

"Yes!" I cry out with bone-deep relief as I feel myself open around his invasion, but in the next moment I have to brace my hands against the tree-trunk, my pleasured outburst turning to deep grunts. He shoves his entire mass into me in that first, brutal thrust of his hips, flattening me against the tree with strength that far surpasses mine.

I have never, *ever,* been wrenched open like this, and had he not prepared me, my screams would be from agony. As it is, I grit my teeth against the massive intrusion, feeling him spread me open far wider and deeper than any man before him. But he is *alpha,* and my body adjusts to him because every instinct hot-wired into my DNA recognizes that he will accept nothing but complete submission.

He growls over me, behind me, forcing my weeping womb to coat his thick cock in even more liquids with the noise that vibrates from his chest into my back and down to my very core. I shudder in his grasp, moaning with forced pleasure when he rolls his hips against mine. There is no denying the *need* I have for this, nor how unbelievable it feels. I have a fleeting thought of finally understanding the women who shamelessly throw themselves at any alpha they meet, before I have to dig my fingers into the bark and bite down on a scream. He's picking up speed, battering my pussy into submission with each and every thrust, his grunts of pleasure accentuating the yelps that escape through my gritted teeth.

I have almost adapted to his rhythm when he shifts the bruising grip on my hips, one hand moving in front of my body where I'm pressed against the tree. He reaches his goal—my throbbing clit—and my world shatters. He rubs it roughly, just the way I need him to, and I lose all ability to hold myself upright.

"Please, please, please," I sob when he pauses the deep pounding to shift his grip on me. "Don't stop, please, *please!*" My pussy clamps down on his rigid cock and attempts to stimulate him into continuing the unrelenting ravaging. I arch backwards, pressing myself down so far on him that my cervix protests at the depth.

"Please, I *need* you!"

An iron band closes around my torso, underneath my breasts, propping me up against the tree despite my legs' failing support. Once again his nimble fingers dance over my clit, faster and faster despite my wailing demands that he also fuck me, until every muscle in my body *clenches*.

Only then does he move.

The orgasm his skilled hands have pushed me to the edge of crashes over me like a cave-in with the first, brutal thrust into my quivering pussy, and every one that follows brings me higher. I clamp so hard around him I'm sure my release will force him to still, but no matter my body's desperate efforts at containing the climax he only drives in harder. I cry, I scream, I beg for more as well as an end. My nails break on the roughened bark I desperately claw at, but only when he finally, *finally,* shouts out in a guttural outburst and freezes deep inside of me is my body allowed to ebb.

I sag in his arms, too spent to worry about the semen pulsing against my cervix, and moan softly with the small tremors of aftershock while I come down.

My mind is so exhausted, preoccupied with gasping in enough oxygen to not pass out and the small bursts of pleasure still firing through my nerve endings, that I don't register the growing tension between my legs before the alpha grunts and wraps both arms tighter around my torso, shifting his hips a little so he can press in deeper.

Something big and dense is forced further into my abused pussy, spreading me wider as it continues to grow than even the alpha's punishing cock, and it is not a pleasant sensation. I gasp and struggle to get free, but he keeps me still against his form with arms as unmovable as if they were carved from granite, making shushing noises into my hair when *it* hooks behind my pelvic bone and I keen in distress.

It's his knot, my rational side realizes with a start; the swelling gland at the bottom of his member designed to lock me in place for increased chances of fertilization.

"Why are you knotting me?" I want to scream it at him, because the lust that made me spread and Present has been quelled and I want him out of my body. I want out of this park, out of the nightmare that's closing in on me again now that the pleasure has ebbed, but I am knotted so thoroughly I can't even move without my pelvis protesting painfully, tied to an alpha I don't know.

Before I can stop it a sob claws its way out from my compressed chest, bringing with it all the fear and agony I have been suppressing since he came out of the darkness to save me. Tears blur my vision of my desperate nail marks in the tree I've been fucked up against for the past half hour and I let out a low wail as despair so deep it feels like I cannot contain it takes over my limp body. There are no words forming in my mind to phrase why I am shaking wretchedly in the prison of his arms, only a deep, black sensation spreading through my chest and arms threatening to swallow me whole.

He never answers me, but when I start to cry he shifts us both, kneeling down on the dirty ground so I am sat on his lap, cradled against his chest.

And then the most wonderful sound I've ever heard rumbles out from his chest, deep and loud. It penetrates my very bones, makes my teeth tingle and my muscles melt. It's an alpha purr—a *real* alpha purr. His gift to me in return for what I offered him.

The empty blackness releases its hold on me, retreating when utter *calm* washes through my sore body. His presence inside of me becomes tolerable as my muscles slowly relax, and when his one, oversized hand finds the small swelling on my stomach where his knot is locked, rubbing gently against my shirt, I sigh with pleasure. The soft stimulation coaxes my channel to give in to the pressure, allowing peace to filter from my body to my mind.

My eyes flutter closed. I make myself more comfortable against him, resting my scraped and bleeding fingers on the arm he has wrapped around me and the hand that continues to rub slow circles over my stomach. Some primitive part of me understands that by assuming this position, with his back turned to the open park behind us, he is letting himself be vulnerable to attacks in order to ensure my comfort. He could turn around to make sure no one can sneak up on us, but that would mean I'd be facing the bloody mess of broken bodies. So he doesn't.

He doesn't even stop the loud purring that must be audible far into the darkness surrounding us once I settle down. It keeps vibrating soothingly through me from everywhere we are touching, allowing me to find pleasure and comfort in the sensation of the steady stream of semen I can feel leaking into me. As long as I don't think, my hormones and instincts keep me placid and content.

It takes more than half an hour before the knot starts to retract, and fifteen more minutes before it is soft enough that he can withdraw from my swollen pussy without hurting me.

He lifts me off his lap by the hips and a river of fluids flushes out of me, covering him in a sticky mess. He doesn't seem fazed though, and quickly zips up his pants before getting to his feet, pulling me with him.

I stagger, every muscle in my body protesting wildly at having to carry my own weight again, but I manage to find my footing and drag up my nearly ruined pants before I turn around to face him.

The killer.

I let a killer fuck me. Knot me. I even freaking *Presented* for him.

The silence is deafening in the absence of his rich purr and I swallow, suddenly nervous again. He is once more a large, looming shadow, and the way he watches me makes me feel like a mouse cornered by a cat.

I find his eyes, searching for his intentions in their depths.

They are icy gray once more, now the pupils aren't blown wide from sexual hunger, but the anger and frustration in them startles me.

He's looking at me as if I am his enemy—as if he didn't just spend the better part of an hour soothing me with his purr while his knot was locked inside of me.

I swallow and take a step back, fear making its way back into my hazed mind. "W-will you hurt me?"

Not the smartest thing to say, perhaps, but the complete change in his demeanor shakes me more than anything else has this evening. For some reason, while he tended to me so carefully after mating with me, I'd forgotten what he was.

That he has fucked me doesn't make me safe, despite whatever primitive mutterings of 'mate' and 'protection' my instincts try to thrust into my conscious mind.

The mountain of a man keeps quiet, gaze locked on my face. He's reading my expression, I think, must see the confusion and fear. I wish I knew what he was thinking.

Slowly, careful to keep my eyes on him, I take a step to the side. When he doesn't move to stop me, I brave voicing the question that can end me.

"Will you let me leave?"

My breath rushes out in a relieved exhale when he nods once. I glance to the muddy ground and the grotesque display of my attackers' mutilated corpses before quickly looking back to him again. He's still watching me.

I wish I knew what he was thinking.

"Thank you,"

His eyes narrow, as if my gratitude is insulting somehow.

Does he think I mean for the sex?

"For letting me leave," I clarify, shifting nervously further toward the bushes behind us. My foot presses against *something,* and I can only guess as to what it is. I don't look down. "And for ... saving me."

For the first time he breaks eye contact, gaze sweeping over the ground as he surveys the damages. I take the opportunity to move closer to my promised freedom, not quite willing to turn my back on him just yet. If he changes his mind I want to see it coming.

"If I see you alone after dark again, you won't like the consequences."

I jump at the dark voice that rings from his shadowed form, my eyes widening in shock at the threat.

"Do you understand?" he asks, taking one step closer to my now shaking body.

I do.

Unable to keep my reawakened fear under control any longer I turn around, and I run. The burn of his eyes on my back follows me as I flee the darkened river bank.

SIX

TWO WEEKS LATER

The darkness slowly recedes as I blink the blur from my eyes in an effort to shake away the same dream that's been haunting me for two weeks now.

The same nightmare, I correct myself. My breathing is still huffing out of my chest in quick, shallow gasps, and my sheets are sticking to my sweat-covered skin.

Annoyed with myself for the warm aching for attention between my thighs I kick my covers off and roll out of bed to get dressed before I can reach for a vibrator and shame myself even further.

Two weeks.

It's been two weeks since I was saved by a dangerous killer. Two weeks since I Presented for him and allowed him to take me on a darkened river bank like a common whore.

On wobbly legs I make my way to the bathroom to

splash some cold water on my face, severing the lingering echo of the dream. *Nightmare. For fuck's sake!*

I glare angrily at my face in the mirror as the cold water droplets trickle down my neck, slowly cooling off my overheated body. The wide, fearful eyes staring back look like they belong to a lost little girl.

And that's the most infuriating part.

Knowing what I allowed him to do is bad enough—hell, it could probably fuel a few years' worth of therapy visits, if I was stupid enough to ever tell anyone, but *this*... This constant and unrelenting yearning for a man I don't even know, an alpha who thought nothing of knotting me surrounded by corpses of men he'd slain... It feels like being betrayed by my own mind, my own body.

If only I would stop dreaming about that night I might be able to forget and pretend like it never happened. But every night I relive the memory of being in that damned park with him, of his hands touching me in every sweet spot and... and his knot locking inside of me.

I blush and drop my gaze, not wanting to look even myself in the eyes while remembering the sweet agony of being tied with an alpha.

Before him, I never truly understood why some women chase after any alpha that happens to cross her path. They are all arrogant and self-assured, completely unshakable in the knowledge that all the power in society belongs to them. They take what they want and are insufferably overbearing with the female gender, most seemingly viewing us as just another possession to conquer.

It wasn't until that stranger's brutal knot locked deep inside of me and his purr soothed my fears that I knew why any woman would be interested in them.

Now, I get it, because every time I think about what it felt like to be tied with such a powerful male, my sex softens as if to prepare me, and my heart rate spikes. On some base and primitive level, I want him to do it again.

I turn away from the mirror, as disgusted with myself as I always am first thing in the morning these days. The lingering cobwebs of my lurid dreams make the memory of his touch way too strong, and my shame along with it.

Thankfully, there's a cure, even if it's only temporary.

I stalk to the kitchen and load up my beloved coffee machine, fully prepared to drown my shameful memories in caffeine and the clarity brought along by the daylight peeping in through my windows. Once the coffee is brewed I sip it while it's still near-scalding, sighing with relief as the caffeine works its magic on my foggy head and the last remnants of the dream disappear.

There. My mind and body once again belong to me, and I have work to do.

IT TURNS out that being as-good-as-unemployed when you're basically living paycheck to paycheck is an excellent way of finding out just how low you'll sink in order to eat.

I used to be very proud of my reporting career. I

fought my way through college working three part time jobs, seeing how my parents weren't exactly inclined- nor capable of helping me, and when I got the job as junior reporter for one of the biggest newspapers in town, I was sure all the demeaning jobs of my college days were past me.

As I type away at my $0.0005/word web article on grout cleaning, I do my very best to push back the festering resentment toward my senior editor, Roy, who so unceremoniously suspended me—without pay, mind you—two weeks ago. It's not like I *chose* to Present in the middle of that stupid press conference!

Heat floods my cheeks at the humiliating memory. Okay, so maybe Roy didn't have much of a choice, seeing how every politician in the city threatened to boycott the paper for all eternity if he didn't get rid of me. Not that they knew the girl who Presented in their midst and caused them to launch into an all-out brawl by name, but the staffer who'd rescued me had apparently told them which newspaper my press badge said I was from.

A sudden, loud knock on my door interrupts my thoughts, making me jump and flail so violently I nearly tip my refilled mug.

Maybe it's Roy come to give me my job back.

Even as my stomach clenches with hope at the thought, I know it's not. Even if *'the incident'* wasn't still being referred to every time the Liberals' Peter Leod appeared on the screen, I doubt very much that anyone wants to see my face again until after the election.

A delivery guy stands in the hallway outside my 4th floor apartment, holding a large white box in expensive-looking cardboard out toward me. On top balances a thick envelope and a smaller box.

"Miss Adams?" he says, looking my disheveled figure up and down.

I wrap my cardigan closer around my sweatpants and food-stained t-shirt. "Yeah, that's me."

"Delivery for you." Without missing a beat he shifts the small tower of parcels to one hand, balancing them nimbly while he pulls out a machine for me to sign my name.

I do, clasping onto the packages with both hands as soon as I am done. It isn't often I get anything but bills in the door. "Who's it from?"

"I ain't in the detective business, ma'am," the delivery guy says, turning back around now that his job here is done. "But it's a special delivery. Make of that what you will."

I stare after him for two more seconds, before curiosity finally wins out and I slam the door shut to inspect the packages.

That it is a special delivery tells me about as much as the ivory cardboard and heavy paper envelope does—that whoever sent it has enough money to throw away on postage and packaging.

I glance at the envelope, but excitement I vaguely remember from Christmas when I was little makes me reach for the small package first.

It's made from the same ivory cardboard as the larger package. I brush my fingertips around the edge. lift the lid —and frown.

Inside is a beautiful, golden mask with black feathers and shimmery stones adorning the sides and rim of the eye holes.

"What the...?" I'd half expected it to be some form of fancy pastries or cupcakes, judging by the white packaging.

With less grace I hurriedly rip the lid off the larger box—and find a pile of silky, black fabric. A dress. A *very* pretty dress with a full, silk skirt—far above anything I'd ever be able to afford myself, even if I weren't currently trying to make a living off questionable content writing.

Hoping for an explanation I tear open the letter, but if anything, it just leaves me with more questions.

> Dear Miss Adams,
> You are hereby invited to the annual charity masquerade at Town Hall, October the 19th at 7pm.

The short note is handwritten on thick, white paper to match the envelope, but there is no signature or any other distinguishing features to help me determine the sender's identity.

Included in the envelope is a golden ticket with my name and the date written on it in intricate print, presumably what will allow me entry to the famed masquerade.

Every year the political elite and socialites of Mattenburg dress up in fanciful costumes to congratulate each other on their wealth and power, while compensating for the glitzy affair by claiming it's all for charity.

At least, that's what I assume goes on, because no one outside of the elite is ever allowed inside, not even the press. And yet here I am, with a literal golden ticket in my hand. Someone's sent me not only an invite to the most exclusive event of the year, but a beautiful costume to go along with it.

But *why?*

I am no one important, and a reporter to boot. In as long as the masquerade has existed, not a single reporter has managed to sneak into this exclusive event. Whoever's behind this must know what my job is.

So why are they trying to get me in?

A cold chill travels down my back when the thought of how exactly I might have drawn the attention of someone powerful enough to orchestrate this.

The only thing that sets me apart from any other reporter in this city is that *I* am the one who nearly caused a riot among the top politicians. The same people who will undoubtedly be present at the masquerade.

Is someone hoping I'll do the same at this event?

But why? There won't be any cameras present, so even if I did Present again there wouldn't be any proof like there was at that damned press conference.

I shudder at the thought. There wouldn't be any

proof, but there likely wouldn't be anyone to save me, either.

As much as a very large part of me is giddy with excitement over the chance to be the first reporter to gain access to the annual masquerade, I can't help but think back to the two times I've lost control around alphas. If it were just the once, I could believe it was just a freak accident, but...

A ghostly touch of a large, powerful man's intimate caress echoes in my mind, and I shove the boxes away with an involuntary spasm. If I could Present to a stranger, a masked killer no less, then who's to say it won't happen again? Clearly, my biology is all haywire, and if there's one thing I don't need, it's another humiliating encounter with a roomful of alphas.

No, whoever sent me that dress and invitation has wasted their money. As much as I'd love to get the exclusive inside scoop on the masquerade, it isn't worth the risk.

Resolute, I shove the boxes to the side with my foot and walk back to my computer. I've got grout cleaning instructions to write, and bills to pay, and I'm not getting stuck any further into politics before the election is well and truly over. The end. Case closed.

My fingers hover over the keyboard as I glance back at the magnificent, black silk dress.

Of course... if I *were* to go and get the inside scoop, Roy would have no choice but to reinstate me... And probably give me a significant raise.

I look back at my computer screen, biting my lip as I

stare at tip number five for achieving sparkling clean grouts.

But if I don't take this chance, then can I really call myself a proper reporter? If I'm too scared to take the biggest opportunity I'll ever see in my entire career, do I even deserve to get my job back?

SEVEN

That the media isn't allowed inside for the masquerade doesn't mean they're not covering the year's biggest event.

When my taxi pulls up a little down the street the flashes of cameras and buzz of excitement from Town Hall's main entrance light up the evening sky, and I can see a throng of people gathered around what I know to be the red carpet leading the way inside.

"Shouldn't you be in a limo?" my driver asks as he glances back at me through the rear view mirror.

I probably should, but there isn't exactly room for fancy transportation in my budget, and whoever my fairy godmother is, they forgot to send a pumpkin along with the dress.

"Everyone does limos," I say, in my best socialite-imitation. "Where's the fun in that?"

I throw money at the cab driver before he can question why I've got him dropping me off down the street if

I'm trying to make an entrance, and quickly step out onto the pavement. My dress, as beautiful as it is, is a bit of a nightmare to straighten out, and I stumble in my heels as I try to undo any wrinkles caused by the taxi drive.

"Careful now." Strong hands clasp around my waist, steadying me before I manage to fall on my face.

I squeak in shock over the unexpected touch, causing the owner of said hands to emit a rumbling laugh.

"Sorry, lovely. I didn't mean to startle you."

I whip my head up just in time to see my large, tux-dressed rescuer release his grip on me and offer me a charming smile from underneath his black mask.

A shock of deja-vu makes me gasp out loud, but the flash of recognition is gone the second my brain catches up. This man might be an alpha, judging from his sheer size and authoritative aura, but he's not the same man my startled mind first saw. This one isn't dressed in black, hi-tech fabric, and his mask is clearly ornamental, not something a thug would wear to commit a crime. No, everything about this man oozes high society, and I need to get my head screwed on straight or I might as well give up my hope of getting my old job back and go home right now.

"Sorry, I didn't see you there," I offer, giving him a quick smile. "Thanks for the rescue."

"Always a pleasure to save a damsel in distress." From the playful tone of his voice I can tell he's joking, and my responding grin is involuntary.

"May I escort the lady in?" he asks, holding out his

arm for me. "If I am not too bold in presuming you're going to the masquerade, as well?"

I touch my ornate mask and flash him another smile. I was planning on sliding unseen up the stairs and through security with as little attention as possible, but... perhaps arriving with someone who clearly belongs there isn't the worst idea.

Tentatively, I place my hand on his arm. "Sure, that would be great."

An odd sort of smile plays on his lips as he looks down at me, but it's gone before I can contemplate it further. He leads me toward the flashing crowd of photographers and journalists, walking slowly enough that I can keep up in my heels, and I feel more than a little thankful he's decided to accompany me through the throng. Something about his self-assured presence takes the edge off my nerves, and when the gathered media turn their attention on us as we step onto the red carpet, he easily fends off their questions with that charming smile of his while somewhat shielding me from the many flashes.

"You've done this before," I say as we walk up the steps toward the main doors and away from the crowd.

"I have," he admits, his easy smile never leaving those sensuous lips. "An unfortunate downside of my job, you might say."

"Yeah, real unfortunate that," I say, not managing to catch my snarky commentary before it's escaped my lips.

But my companion only laughs his deep, rumbly

laugh again and gives me an amused side-glance. "My my, you're as mouthy as you are lovely. How refreshing."

I arch an eyebrow at his relatively gentle flirting, considering he's an alpha, but it's shielded by my mask and he doesn't see it. Instead, he turns his attention at the two burly alphas guarding the door. I spot guns in both their belts.

"Good evening, gentlemen," my companion says as he produces a golden ticket from his pocket, before turning to me. "I do hope you remembered yours, my lovely?"

I jolt and reach for my purse. It seems like it takes forever for my jittery fingers to undo the clasp and produce my own ticket, the deafening silence from the two guards not helping matters.

When I finally do manage to get it out, the left-most alpha snatches it from my hand and scrutinizes it so closely I'm sure he knows I don't belong.

Thankfully, he passes it back to me with a grunt before my heart manages to skip out of my throat.

"Go on in."

"Well, aren't they a couple of cheerful fellas," I mumble under my breath as my companion leads me through the door.

"They're hired to be a bit rough around the edges," he says as we step into the main hall, and my mouth drops open. "You wouldn't believe the attempts some reporters go through to counterfeit one of those tickets."

"Uh-huh." Perhaps if I hadn't been so gobsmacked by the golden sea of decadence surrounding us, I would have flinched at the mention of reporters trying to sneak in, but I'm too busy trying to take everything in to pay his comment much mind.

All around us are people dressed in beautiful robes, with so many strings of diamonds around their necks it's surprising they can keep their heads up. Waiters carry flutes of champagne and canapés around, skillfully avoiding the mingling guests with fluid motions. Everyone's wearing extravagant masks, and pealing laughter echoes through the large hall.

The level of wealth on display here is staggering. No wonder they don't want the press to see—if the public knew how they flaunt their riches at this so-called charity event, there'd be a riot.

"It's positively disgusting, isn't it?" Judging by my companion's teasing smile, he must have noticed my open-mouthed stare. "Makes you wonder how many street kids could be fed and sheltered if we all just stayed home and spent a fraction of the cost of this event on the charity we all claim we're here to support."

"So why don't you?" Is he trying to bate me to admit I don't belong here? For the first time, I wonder if I would recognize the face behind his black mask.

"Power," he says easily. "I need it, and it's here in spades. It's the paradox of politics—we all hate each other, but to gain a foothold we have to play these pompous games of gilded pleasantries. Is that not why you're here, darling? The draw of power?"

I stare up at him, denial withering on my lips. I'm here

for the same reason all those reporters are gathered at the door—to get a glimpse of the rich and powerful, and—hopefully—a taste as well. That my goal is to get my job back doesn't negate the fact that I need this epicenter of power to get it, just as much as any politician needs it for his connections.

"I suppose you could say that," I admit, finally moving my gaze from his to scout across the crowd of people. "But if people knew..."

"If people knew how we flaunted our wealth like peacocks in here, while so many starve out there?" he continues when I trail off, and despite the smoothness of his voice, I get the distinct impression there is an edge to it that wasn't there before. "Well, my dear, that's why we go to such great lengths to keep spying eyes out."

I nod without looking at him, not entirely sure I won't crack under his scrutinizing gaze at that comment.

Spying eyes, indeed. It dawns on me that whoever sent me that invitation must have known what could happen if a reporter got inside this ball. Who with enough power to get me on the guest list would want to risk the uproar from the masses that is bound to happen if the true nature of our society's gap in wealth is finally displayed for all to see?

"Peter."

I turn toward the sound of a male voice, to see a masked man in a tux slide up beside my companion and place a hand on his shoulder. "They're waiting for you."

"I'll be right there," the alpha next to me rumbles. He

turns to me and offers an apologetic smile. "I'm afraid duty calls."

Peter? Surely not…

"Peter Leod?" I ask, because I can't stop myself. There is no way my masked partner is the Liberal Party's Crown Prince. The Crown Prince who nearly got dethroned thanks to me. Peter is a common enough name, I don't even know why my first reaction to hearing it would be to think he might be *that* Peter…

My internal denial dies in a fizz when the large alpha by my side gives me a decidedly wicked wink, bends his head and presses a butterfly soft kiss to the back of my hand.

"I hope your first masquerade is an enjoyable experience."

And then he turns and walks away from me, his tall figure easily cutting through the throng of people until he disappears in the golden sea of decadence.

Wow.

I just had a casual chat with Peter Leod about inequality and the city's power structure.

And if he knew who I was, he'd likely pay good money to have me murdered.

He might be a Liberal, but I have no delusions that the power elite on the left side of the middle isn't as brutally ruthless as the current Lord Mayor.

"Ladies and Gentlemen—if I may have your attention for a moment, please."

The booming voice from further in the hall draws my

thoughts from Leod to the masked man who stands in front of the double doors I know lead into Town Hall's magnificent ball room. I've only ever been there as part of a press tour, of course, never an actual ball. Until tonight.

"As you may be aware, this year's ball is in support of Mattenburg's Home for Destitute Children, so once the traditional auction starts I do encourage you to open your hearts—and your wallets. But, as much as I know you will be thinking of the poor orphans, let's not forget that tonight is the one night a year we get to take a step back from our responsibilities as Mattenburg's rightful rulers. Tonight, we drink, we dance... and we fuck. Welcome to the Masquerade!"

Wait, what? *Fuck?!* I stare around the room, open-mouthed, to see if anyone else is as flabbergasted as I at *that* development, but no one seems to so much as bat an eyelid. When the double doors swing open behind the man who's just welcomed us in rather disturbing fashion, he sidesteps—and everyone pours in like willing sheep to the slaughter.

God, I hope I'm not going to regret this. Hesitantly, I follow the throng of people. When I pass the widely smiling host, I see the Mayor's chain glinting around his neck. Lord Mayor Bremen, of course. He's looking over the crowd as we pass him to get into the ballroom, smiling and nodding at a few guests he must recognize despite their masks.

But the second I pass through the doors, my mind is thoroughly taken off the Lord Mayor.

The last time I saw this ballroom, it was a beautiful piece of neo-Gothic architecture, with its domed ceiling, dark-tiled floor and sweeping balconies, but it was nowhere near the level of decadence I see before me now.

Now, the floor seems to have been laid with intricate patterns of gold leaf, the crystal chandeliers high above setting the whole room aglow as they reflect in it. Beautifully set, round tables fill up the room, and they too—along with their chairs—seem like they've been covered in gold leaf patterns. Even the large flower arrangements centered on each one have been dusted in gold.

On the Eastern side of the room is what appears to be a stage curtained in thousands of beads glowing in jewel shades, and I can't help but wonder if they're true gemstones.

"May I please see your ticket, miss?"

I jolt at the gentle touch to my arm and whip my head around to the speaker. It's a black-and-white clad young man with a finely boned, attractive face, and for a moment I think my open-mouthed staring has given me away—that it's obvious I don't belong, despite the luxurious dress I was gifted along with my ticket.

"I need to see your ticket number so I can seat you," he explains after a beat of silence.

"Oh! Yes, of course, sorry." I fumble with my purse and pull out the golden paper with my name on it, offering it to the young man.

He glances at the ticket and stretches out an arm toward the back of the room. "This way, miss."

I DON'T RECOGNIZE the five people I'm sharing a table with during dinner, but from the excited chatter around me I can understand that that's a major part of the excitement for most participants of this extravagant masquerade. I try to listen in on their conversation for any hint of reportable news, but the gossip *du jour* is focused on who might be hiding behind which mask, and which family may or may not have funded which political party.

It's not until the end of dessert the night's main event finally unfolds.

"Ladies and gentlemen!"

Every head in the hall snaps toward the stage at the booming voice echoing through the gilded room, and I recognize Bremen on his Mayor's chain once more as he stands on the stage with the now open, jeweled curtains.

"I trust you've all enjoyed your meals and are eager to continue on with the night's festivities. We have secured some fabulous prizes for the highest bidders tonight. Do remember that the proceeds go to Mattenburg's Home for Destitute Children, so don't be stingy now. I promise you, this year's wares are worth that extra bid."

A rush of excited murmuring travels through the crowd before hushed anticipation falls over the hall. I glance to my sides to see if my dinner companions can give me any clue as to why a mere charity auction has everyone this wound up, but I needn't have bothered.

On the stage, the spotlight on the Lord Mayor dims

and the curtains fall forward with a trickling sound, hiding him from view. But seconds later, they're withdrawn again, and I can make out vague figures in the darkness.

The flash of spotlights reveals what's on sale this evening.

A row of young, naked men and women stand on the stage, eighteen of them. A chain attached to iron collars link them all together.

My stomach roils as the implication of what's about to happen sets in with a shock of horror, and it's all I can do to swallow my disgusted cry so to not blow my cover.

The masquerade's main event is a slave auction!

"Can we have the first item on the list step forward?"

The tux-clad man calling out from the podium next to the stage isn't the Lord Mayor himself, but his mask hides his identity.

Another man, dressed in white, walks across the stage to the left-most naked man on display, and deftly detaches his chain from the young woman to his side. He gives it a tug, and the young man on the other end follows him to the center of the stage.

"This fine young stag is twenty-two years old and in prime condition," the presenter says, as if he's describing a prize cow. The white-clad man with the chain in his hand makes him turn to display his smooth, muscular body. He's no alpha, but he's obviously a fit young man. A golden sheen reflects off his skin as he is made to pose for the audience, and when the white-clad man pulls his flaccid penis forward to show it off he only flinches once before resuming his stone-faced stare at some point above the crowd.

"He may not have a knot for you ladies to enjoy, but I'm told he's very skilled with his tongue. Shall we start the bids at $10,000?"

As the bidding for the first young soul begins, I get up from my seat. I'm careful not to make much noise, but I needn't have bothered being discrete. Every last one of my dinner companions are staring up at the stage with rapt attention, oblivious to what's going on around them.

I'm fortunate that I'm seated at the very back, because no one else notices me as I tiptoe to the nearby stairs leading up to the balconies overlooking the ballroom.

My first instinct was to try and put a stop to this monstrosity, but I quickly realized I could do nothing for the poor people currently displayed on-stage like pieces of meat. I have no doubt the Chief of Police is seated somewhere in the crowd, eyes glued to naked flesh like every other piece of shit down there.

The only thing I can do is document what's happening here and let the world know just what kind of depraved monsters we let rule our city.

The balcony I find offers a perfect view of the ballroom and stage. I press myself in behind a pillar and fish out my phone with shaking hands. Then, I press *'record'* and aim it at the stage.

Below me, the young man has been sold to a middled-aged woman in a green-and-black dress while I climbed the stairs. He is led to her by the chain around his neck, and made to kneel in front of her.

I feel sick as she grabs his offered chain and pulls her skirts open, displaying her bared crotch for the whole room to see. A hard yank on the chain, and the young man's face presses in between her thighs. Cheers erupt from the tables around them.

"Next up is this lovely young woman. She's twenty-one, and she's never taken a knot before, but I'm sure we'll change that tonight, won't we, gentlemen?"

I grit my teeth as the presenter has a brunette girl display herself on stage. The bids are even more aggressive than earlier, and a couple of alpha growls rise above the guests.

When she is finally sold to a huge alpha on the northern side of the room I have to steady myself on the balcony's banister to find the strength to keep filming. No sooner has she been delivered to her new owner before he clears half the table with a swing of his arm, presses her over it and paws at her small sex like a barely-contained beast.

His cock is out, and the sight of its hugeness has flashes of memories flickering in my brain. Of being pressed up against a tree in a dark, abandoned park. A stranger behind me, forcing his much too big cock up inside of me…

When the alpha below mounts his female, her squeal rocks through me like a physical force. But it's no longer anger at the depravity on display that makes me shake like a leaf in the wind.

No, it's something far worse than that.

The alpha ruts on top of the young woman below, sparing her nothing as she keens and grasps at the tablecloth for purpose, her legs kicking on each side of his powerful hips. All around the other guests stare with lecherous glee, some openly touching themselves.

And I wish with everything I am that I was back in the arms of the alpha who made me scream like the poor girl trapped on the table in their midst.

I'm so enthralled with the imagery below that I don't notice I'm no longer alone in my hiding spot before a large hand touches my bare shoulder.

"Enjoying the show, darling?"

EIGHT

I spin around so quickly I nearly drop my phone.

My unwanted companion easily catches it before it falls to the ground and deftly turns off the camera.

I stare up at him in utter horror, my mouth opening and closing of its own accord as I try to come up with a plausible excuse for why I'm lurking in the shadows, videotaping the secret sex slave auction the entire city's elite would undoubtedly do anything to avoid the public ever discovering.

He's an alpha, I recognize, partly from his size and partly from the way my already awakened ovaries feel his pheromone's magnetic pull like a physical force. He's masked like everyone else, and dressed in a black tux—like every other alpha here—but there's something... familiar about him.

"I..."

"And just how did you manage to get yourself an invitation, hmm?" he asks in a hushed voice that does nothing to rob him of his natural authority.

"I... don't know," I croak.

His lips twitch. "Somehow I doubt that. You're a reporter, I take it?"

I want to shake my head no, but something in that commanding gaze of his makes me nod before I even realize what I'm doing.

"Brave little girl," he says, and this time there's just the barest hint of a purr in his voice. Almost as if he approves of my courage. "Risking your life for a story."

"It's a little more than just a story," I hiss, some of my previous anger finally resurfacing, now that fear has somewhat quelled my inexplicable desire. "You rape people. You *sell* them!"

He smirks—he actually *smirks*, as if anything about this fucked up situation is amusing in any way, shape or form—and places his large hand back on my shoulder. An unspoken demand for obedience. "I think you'd better come with me."

THE MASKED ALPHA leads me away from the ballroom, through hallways and up a flight of stairs until we stop in front of a dark, wooden door on the second floor.

I gape as I read the name on the little brass plate next to it.

P. Leod, Lib.

This must be his office.

"Peter Leod?" I stutter in utter bewilderment, for the second time this night.

He gives me an easy smile as he unlocks the door and gestures for me to go in. "Lucky for you, yes."

"How can you let something like this happen right in front of you?" I ask, even as I obey his unspoken command. "You're supposed to be all about equality and fairness, but you're just peachy letting those poor men and women get publicly *raped* for you and your buddies' amusement? I knew you politicians were all scumbags, but *this—*"

Leod interrupts my rant by offering me a tumbler filled with amber liquor he's poured from the bottle located on his desk. I take it more on instinct than any desire for alcohol.

"No one's getting raped," he says, his voice as calm and authoritative as when he is in front of the cameras, rallying the adoring masses for his party. "It's a show. The young ladies and gentlemen on stage are paid for their participation, and briefed beforehand. They're made to sign a nondisclosure agreement, of course, but they're there by choice."

"*Choice?* You mean to tell me anyone would *want* to stand naked in front of a bunch of masked pricks, and then have to... in front of all those strangers? Somehow, I find that very hard to believe, *Mr. Leod.*" I don't know why I'm challenging the powerful alpha—if I were any sort of smart, I'd nod and smile, and hope he bought my faked acceptance with all I've got. All I know is that my gut is still clenching with shame at how arousing I found the rough mating, and if I don't protest against the abomination of a *show*, I'm going to lose my dinner right here on Leod's polished floors.

The big alpha sighs lightly and, after pouring himself a tumbler of the amber liquor, sits down in one of the two sleek, gray armchairs that take up most of the space in his office not occupied by the large desk. With his drink-free hand he removes his mask and gestures for me to sit. "Well, I presume most accept because of the money more than a specific desire to get fucked like a whore by a fat one-percenter in a ridiculous costume. But yes—it's consensual. If you'd like, I'll take you down to their changing rooms after the show's over, and you can see for yourself."

I bite my lip as I sit down in the chair in front of Mattenburg's most popular politician. I might have known who he was while he was still wearing his mask, but there is something about being face-to-face with him that has my nervous system on high alert. A flash of memory of his gray eyes boring into mine across the conference room seconds before all hell broke loose just a few weeks ago makes me gulp down a hearty mouthful of what turns out to be smooth whiskey. Yeah, there is no way I am removing *my* mask, on the off chance of him actually remembering the face of the girl who's done serious damage to his reputation right before the election.

"So... you're actually willing to show me around behind the scenes?" I ask, forcing my focus back to the task at hand rather than the disturbing memories of what happened the last time I saw his face in person. "Why?"

He shrugs. "It would benefit no one if you ran a story with false accusations against the city's elite. You'd never work again, and if someone just slightly more sinister than your average politician took enough offense, you possibly wouldn't breathe, either."

"And you care why?" I ask, not bothering to hide my skepticism at his supposed goodwill. "Why don't you just shut me up? Don't get me wrong, I don't particularly *want* to end up floating downriver, but your grandiosity is... surprising."

His full lips pull up in a smirk, and something decidedly devious glints in those cool eyes of his. "So you don't buy the Liberal do-good persona my PR team is so keen on portraying? Pity." He swishes his glass and lets his eyes flicker up and down me for a beat. "I don't particularly enjoy offing pretty girls. Especially not when they could prove useful."

"Useful... how?" I'm not in the greatest position to barter, but images of the naked girl forced down on the dining table with a masked alpha rutting on top of her suddenly flash through my mind. I don't realize my thighs are squeezing together before I see amusement flicker in Leod's gaze as he watches me. Amusement, and just a hint of the kind of heat that has my breath hitching in my throat.

Damn alphas! And damn this particular alpha, with his cool eyes, high cheekbones and sinfully inviting mouth. *God, what's wrong with me?* I never have this kind of reaction to a man, *especially* not a ruthless alpha.

Except for a few weeks ago, my subconscious whispers, and I grit my teeth in a desperate attempt at suppressing the memories of the tall, dark stranger who saved me. And then fucked me so brutally I couldn't walk straight for a week.

"Let's just say that it wouldn't be entirely horrible for my standing in the polls if the public was reminded that I'm still the lesser evil of all the candidates. Say a video of the entire political top salivating to live out their basest alpha urges surfaced tomorrow. I'm sure certain unfortunate footage of myself would practically disappear in the uproar following the public knowledge that all their elected officials really hunger for is ruling every one of you like we did in the stone ages—with our knots."

I take a sip of my glass as I let his words filter through, eying him carefully. It's an odd experience, sitting in front of a man who's made such a name for himself with his moderate views on alphas' natural place at the top. Sure, I never particularly bought into his personal beliefs aligning with his politics, but hearing him talk so blatantly about the nature of his kind is still disconcerting.

"So all alphas really are alike," I whisper, more to myself than him, but his thin smile tells me he's heard me.

"You certainly think so, don't you, little bird? The way

you assumed every one of us would not only accept, but also participate in, the kind of depravity the show seeks to emulate." He cocks his head and sets his tumbler on the desk so he can place his fingertips against each other as he regards me. "We may all have the urge for dominance wired into our DNA, but there *is* a difference, darling. Had Bremen discovered you filming the show, you *would* have ended up downriver. Likely after he'd treated you to the kind of experience the young ladies on stage are enduring as we speak."

I gulp, because the picture he paints of what *could* have happened, had he not been the one to come across my hiding spot, is way too vivid. I don't have to ask to know what he's saying is the truth—Bremen has always been a merciless leader, and I have no doubt that what goes on away from the public's eye is far more sinister than I have any desire ever to experience.

"So... you *want* me to publish this video?" I ask. I'm proud of the lack of shaking in my voice.

He nods a single time in confirmation.

I draw in a deep breath to steel myself for the question I've been pondering ever since he let me into his office.

"Mister Leod... did *you* give me that ticket?"

Both his eyebrows draw up high on his forehead. "Your entry ticket? No. But I find it curious that you don't know who gifted you the arguably most valuable asset a reporter can obtain in Mattenburg these days. Someone must like you an awful lot. Or potentially—want something from you badly enough they've gone to great lengths ensuring you're in substantial debt to them."

I feel the blood drain from my cheeks—I hadn't considered that angle before now. What if whoever gifted me the dress and golden ticket is going to come collect one of these days?

Shit. Now's not the time to panic about that—not when I've still got a job to do. I need to get the scoop first —and then fret about what, if anything, I'll have to do in return.

"I'm pretty sure that if you were presented with an opportunity of this magnitude, you'd take it, too, and consequences be damned, Mr. Leod," I said, straightening my back and squaring my shoulders.

His smile turns slightly wider. "Naturally."

"Well, it's natural for me, too. And speaking of... I believe you said you'd show me around the auction-participants' dressing room?" I scoot forward on my chair and put my glass of barely-touched whiskey on the desk next to his abandoned tumbler in what I hope is an assertive manner.

Another flicker of amusement in Leod's eyes makes me think that I'm not exactly managing to put on any sort of imposing air, but he humors me nonetheless and gets to his feet with enviable agility. "Yes, I believe I did. Shall we?"

He holds out his hand to help me up, and I try to ignore the warmth from his palm shooting through my skin in electric little bursts as he draws me up next to him. Down low in my abdomen something heats in response.

It's a short change between us, that faint rush of air above me as he draws in a breath that makes me look up—and it's like the cool, calm politician has been replaced with someone else entirely.

Dark heat flames at the back of his gaze with a yearning that echoes through my body to the most primitive parts. I shudder, and his nostrils flare in response. Scenting me, testing the air for my pheromones.

My mouth feels dry as I open it to try and say something, but no words come as I stare up at the looming alpha. Only wet, warm heat down low in my belly, and an insane urge to stretch up so I can lick at his neck.

A sharp knock on the door breaks through my trance before I can do something unforgivably stupid.

"Come in!" Leod practically growls it out, his voice rougher than I've ever heard it before.

Someone steps through the door behind me. When I twist my neck to see who it is, I am greeted by a disdainful look from a tux-clad man in a black mask. Possibly the same one who fetched Leod earlier, but his outfit is so non-distinct and most of his face hidden, so it's impossible to say.

"Oh, for goodness' sake," he hisses without preamble. "You're due on stage for your speech in five minutes, your entire staff is running around like headless chickens looking for you, and then I find you hiding away with a damn floozy in your office? This is *not* what your reputation needs, Peter. You know the Conservatives are on the war path—you cannot risk the entire election on some piece of ass."

I'm too stunned that anyone in a subordinate position would talk to the large alpha like that to be insulted by his description of me. Despite Leod's warning growl he doesn't so much as flinch.

"So now I can't even speak to a fucking woman until the damn election is over? You're being ridiculous, Norman. The young lady and I were merely discussing her family's donations to our party."

"Bullshit," Norman says. "The entire room reeks of alpha rut. From the smell of it, if I'd gotten here just five minutes later you'd have had her bent over your desk. There's too much at risk for this nonsense—you're not an adolescent pup, even though you've damn well been acting like it since that fucking press conference."

"That's enough." Leod's growl is low and threatening this time, and apparently it's classed as his *serious tone,* because the smaller man nods and pinches his lips.

"I'd like you to show Miss Dale the performers' changing rooms. Answer her questions, and if she wishes to see anything else, you escort her there. And after she's done, you put her in a taxi. Understood?"

I gape up at Leod, somewhat stunned by his sudden change back from feral alpha to cool, calm and collected politician. He's even managed to give me a fake name without so much as blinking, while most of my brain is still very much fogged up from the sexual tension still lingering in the air.

Leod doesn't spare me a second glance. Once Norman nods his consent, he simply puts my phone on the desk and leaves the room in long strides.

Apparently, our impromptu meeting is over.

NINE

It's half past midnight when I finally make it home.

The comforting sound of my door clicking shut behind me makes me sigh out in relief and lean against it with a groan.

Who knew mingling with the elite was so exhausting?

At least I now know that what Leod claimed was true—they don't actually sell off human beings as sex slaves. They just pretend they do.

Sick fucks.

The short chat I had with a couple of the *performers* confirmed that they were paid for their participation, and were free to leave after the so-called show. That didn't change the fact that most of them were sporting finger-shaped bruises on their hips and wincing for every step.

I don't bother changing out of my dress as I head for my computer—I just kick off my heels and throw my mask on the desk before I fish my phone out of my purse. Come the morning, every voter in this city is going to know exactly what sort of fantasies the alphas in charge of our society live out under the guise of charity.

THE SMALL DIGITAL clock on my computer shows three-thirty in the morning when I press send on my email to Roy, my editor. I know he usually starts his day at four in the morning, so it won't be long before my article is plastered across the front page, and the video I shot uploaded to the Internet.

My eyes are sore from the late hour and staring so intently at a screen for the past two hours, and I rub them with a yawn, smearing my mascara. Despite everything, I am pretty damn pleased with myself. The article will be run under a pseudonym to avoid retaliation, but I no longer have to fear for my continued employment. In fact, I'm probably getting a promotion and a hefty raise.

A soft knock on my front door startles me out of the fantasy of the cruise I'm going to take once my next paycheck comes in, and I scramble to my feet.

Who the hell knocks at this time of night?

Cautiously, I walk over to my entrance hall and peer out the spyhole. The stairway outside is lit as usual, but I can't see anyone through the small circle. Frowning, I ensure the chain's secure on the door before I open it a few inches.

"Hello?"

Instead of an answer, a large hand slaps against the outside of the door and shoves, ripping the handle out of my palm and breaking the chain as the door flies open wide.

I shriek in shock, only to have a warm hand clapped over my mouth as the masked man who now takes up my entire doorway grabs my wrists with his free hand and pushes me in further.

Once he's inside, he shoves the door closed with his hip without releasing his grip on me, a small smirk playing at the corner of his mouth.

"Hello, my beautiful."

I stare up at him with wide eyes, panic allowing recognition to filter through much slower than it otherwise would.

He's so obviously an alpha, with deviously curved lips and cold eyes, and an all-too-familiar mask covering most of his face. It's not the kind of mask all the high-society people at the masquerade wore. No, it's the kind a man dons to commit crimes without his victims ever learning his identity.

And I've seen him before.

Not even the mask could obscure my memory of that mouth against my neck, nor his broad hands on my hips.

The man from the park—the alpha who had me up against a tree while dead bodies lay strewn at our feet.

"If you promise not to scream, I'll let go," he purrs.

My heart is racing in my chest, and I very much do want to scream for help, but I also don't want to test his temper. From the swiftness with which he killed my attackers, I don't want to gamble on whether or not my neighbors could—or would—react in time.

Slowly, without taking my eyes off him, I nod.

"Good girl." The intruder releases his hold on my wrists and removes his hand from my mouth.

We stare at each other in silence for a moment, until his eyes flick up and down my body in lazy appreciation.

"Knew that dress would look gorgeous on you."

My jaw drops in utter disbelief. "You... *you* sent it?"

"I did." He smiles, but it's a predatory sort of smirk, and I take an involuntary step back. "The dress, the mask... the ticket."

"Why? *How?*" How on Earth does a criminal like him have the sort of connections it would take to get me invited without anyone realizing I didn't belong there?

He takes a step forward, encroaching on my personal space once more as he looks down at me with that unmistakable heat in his eyes. Down low in my abdomen, I can feel the same traitorous something that nearly made me give in to Leod awaken.

When his fingertip touches my chin, small tingles of sensation shoot through my skin and make my nipples tighten.

"A courting gift, sweetling. Perhaps such a thing would usually come before the beautiful present you gave *me*, but I have no intention of shortchanging you."

I blink. Twice. "A... a *courting* gift? You must be out of your mind!" The last part I hiss at him, despite my lingering fear of his looming presence, because the implication of this stranger giving me a *courting gift* is too insane to ignore.

I've heard of women receiving such a thing from an alpha they were seeing. It's another ridiculously old fashioned tradition ingrained into their primitive DNA of wanting to prove to a woman that they can provide for her. It's something given to a female they want to keep by their side—not the stranger they fucked silly in a dark park before going their separate ways.

The intruder bends his head until our breaths mingle, but instead of pressing his lips to mine he runs his nose along the side of my neck, creating goosebumps in his wake. It's all I can do not to pant, and I grit my teeth in a desperate attempt at controlling myself. *No. This is not going to happen again!*

"You Presented for me. You accepted my gift," he whispers into my ear, his hot breath caressing my skin. "You belong to me."

At that, my sense of reality finally snaps back into place with a *twang,* and I take several steps away from him, mouth open in outrage.

"This is not the fucking fifties, dude! I don't *belong* to anyone, least of all some crazy murderer! If you think you can just force your way into my home and I'll yield like a swooning virgin, then you really are out of your mind!"

"*'Crazy murderer'?*" He straightens up from his prowl, but doesn't advance on me again. "Are you referring to the brutes I killed to save you from getting savaged like a piece of meat?"

Despite his words, his voice is still calm and deep, almost soothing to listen to.

"Y-you *knotted* me! In a cold park, while I was still in shock from being attacked, with freaking *corpses* all over the ground!" I sling at him, fisting my hands by my sides as I finally allow myself to vent my anger and frustration from that night.

"I did," he agrees, and then he takes a step forward. And another. Like a prowling panther he stalks toward me, not stopping as I begin to back up. When my back hits the wall, he cages me in with a strong arm coiled with thick muscle on each side of my shoulders.

"After you Presented yourself to me, begging for my knot." He dips his head to my throat again, inhaling deeply. "God, you smell like fucking candy and sex." The last sentence is a deep, rich growl.

I draw in a shaky breath to try and steel myself, but it's ever so hard to think straight with him so close I can practically feel the heat radiating from his body and taste his pheromones on the air. When he licks at my pulse point, I have to bite my lip *hard* to stop a whimper from escaping.

"Begging?" I hiss—or, I try to. It comes out like more of a breathy gasp. "I would never *beg* for that. It hurt!"

He chuckles softly and nuzzles as the side of my neck. "I know, beautiful. It always does, the first time. Tonight will be much more pleasurable for you, I promise."

Hold up!

"What do you mean *'tonight'*?" This time, there's a lot more conviction behind my outrage. I jerk my head to the side so I can give him my best glare. "Look, buddy, I don't know what you think's going to happen here, but I'm *not* sleeping with you!" *Again.* "What happened in that park was a freak accident, okay? I—I was under a lot of stress, and it just *happened*. It doesn't mean you can just knock my door down and claim me like some goddamn caveman!"

The alpha not so much as blinks at my outburst. Hot lips and then teeth press against my throat, nibbling at the tender skin there. "You will let me have you tonight. You will plead and moan for me to please you, and, once I've had my fill of that delicious little cunt of yours, you will take my knot," he hums, not moving his mouth from my throat

My hot blush is as much a reaction to his calm, matter-of-fact tone as it is his crude words, but I don't manage much more than a protesting sputter before he lifts his head to brush his warm, soft lips over mine. Heat envelopes me, from my mouth all the way down through my body to my toes even before his tongue flicks out to trace the seam of my mouth.

When it does, a broken moan cracks out from my lips and is swallowed up by the stranger as he claims my mouth fully.

His kiss is sweet, intoxicating madness, and for those few moments every cell in my body is pure, burning *need*.

Finally, the alpha pulls back an inch, a lazy smirk on his face as I pant hard in front of him.

"Told you." His breath brushes against my face, reminding the primitive part of my brain that he is all alpha.

As if every ounce of my humming body isn't already aware.

However, his arrogance infuriates the other part of me —the part that's always been in control up until I met *him*. That part hates the way he so easily manipulates my hormones into this quivering mess just by *kissing* me. I've been kissed before, and just because this man is an alpha doesn't mean I won't call him on his high-handed mannerisms.

"And why would I let you have me again?" I'm proud that my voice sounds more steady, though I can do nothing about the hoarse note. "I am not going to Present for you—you have no way of tricking me into wanting it this time."

His eyes narrow at my defiance, but he doesn't move any further away. "Is that so?"

I raise my chin with an assurance I don't feel. "Yes. I obviously can't stop you from *forcing* yourself on me, but I will not *let* you do anything to me."

"Hmm," he hums, his head tilting slightly to the side as his gaze burns into mine. "Will you say that if I touch you... right here..." His fingertips suddenly brush up the inside of my thigh, hiking up my dress before slipping in under the fabric of my underwear to skim through the short hair there, "You wouldn't want it?"

My breath hitches in my throat at the sudden intimate caress. Every nerve in my body is alight with sensation. He rubs along my lower lips, teasing me with his fingertips.

"Yes," I croak. Any steadiness has long since left my voice. I should grasp at his hand to push him away, but I'm too startled to move. Instead I just stare up at his storm gray eyes, panting softly into the shared air between us.

"What about here, then?"

His fingers trail up higher, delving in in just the right place. My pelvis jerks out against his touch and I groan involuntarily when he rubs my clit exactly how I like it—firmly, but not too rough.

"Y-yes." I shudder in front of him, unable to keep my thoughts from scattering. It feels too good, and he smells of musk and man and *sex*. My eyes roll back in my head as tendrils of raw pleasure shoot from my greedy clit into the rest of my body.

"Yes, what?" His voice is rougher too, now. Deeper. It isn't exactly helping me keep it together. "Tell me what you want, Leigh."

The sound of my names rolling off his lips in that rough, sultry tone makes my knees buckle. He catches me and presses me up against the wall, rooting my pelvis with his.

What is it I want? *Fuck, I can't think straight!* Not with

that continuous torment of my aching clit and the heat flooding into me from everywhere we're touching. Everything is a haze of desire and *heat,* and he's so damn *close.*

"Tell me you want my cock, sweetling," he whispers. His breath brushes over my face, and then his mouth closes over mine again, pressing against my lips as perfectly as his nimble fingers are pressing against my clit.

My mouth opens for his without hesitation, though the tiny part of my sanity that's still unrestrained by hormones protests wildly. It is soon drowned out by the sweet rush of his tongue dancing against mine.

Right now, there's nothing I want more,

I feel moisture trickle down my spread thighs, readying me for exactly what I've told him I didn't want. The longer he rubs circular motions over my tight little bud and the longer his tongue teases mine deeper and deeper, the more I feel my body giving in, begging for everything his scent is promising me.

The feel of high tech fabric against my palms makes me realize I've grabbed at his shoulders, either for support or submission, but the thought is fleeting, because my climax is fast approaching.

Oh God, I'm about to let him finger me to orgasm right here, in the sanctity of my own home.

The sweet, building ache between my legs doesn't let me fret over such matters. Soon, I am panting into his mouth, my hips pushing rhythmically out against him and my fingers digging into his hard muscles.

Oh yes, so close! So close—

Mere moments before my release the hand underneath my panties slips away and our kiss is broken.

I cry out in frustration, my eyes popping open in time to see the alpha stare down at me expressionlessly.

"What are you doing?" I demand, my tone a lot angrier than I would have dared, had my hormones not been all riled up with desperate need.

I want to punch him. Hard.

"I do believe I am proving a point." Though his face remains neutral, I see desire flicker behind his cool gaze. Desire, and dominance. He wants me to admit what my body has already betrayed, that much is clear.

"Why?" I remove my hands from his shoulders to rub my at my face, not caring if I smear my makeup further. "You could force me if you wanted."

"I could," he agrees, and in the emptiness filling the room now, a trickle flutters up my spine. Of fear, and just the tiniest hint of anticipation.

The silence seems to hang suspended between us for an eternity, but when he finally breaks it, it's not to touch me. Instead, he turns his back to me and lithely walks into my living room, where my computer is still on.

"Clever girl—sending everything off to your editor before morning." His fingertips dance along my keyboard before he turns back around and looks at me. "How much do you think your raise will come to?"

I stare at him, not following this somewhat unexpected jump in conversation. "Uh...?"

"How much do you think it's worth, being the only

reporter to ever get into the annual masquerade? How much do you think any newspaper I'd gone to with this offer would have paid to get what I gave to you? One million dollars? Two?"

Slowly, his intention starts to seep through my still lust-hazed brain. I frown at his masked figure. Surely, he doesn't mean...

My heart begins to pound in my chest. I accepted a gift I should have known was too good to not come with strings attached, and here they are. A debt to the killer who thinks he owns me.

"What do you want from me?" I say, doing my best to project my voice louder than a whisper.

He smiles that cocky half-smile at me. "I should have thought that was plenty clear by now. I want *you*. And I will have you. In return, you shall have this," He turns halfway around again and sweeps an arm toward the darkened windows—toward the city, "The opportunities to make of yourself exactly what you wish. The connections to go as far as you want."

My mouth is suddenly too dry. "Why?" is all I manage to press out through my parched throat.

Why me?

His eyes darken as he stalks back toward me, his face transforming with the devilish expression pulling at his visible features.

"Because from the moment I saw you, I knew you were meant to be mine. And if you weren't so scared of your own instincts, you would know it too. Even now, when you're trying to tell yourself that you're scared of me, that you don't want this... even now do your instincts whisper the truth to you. You Presented for me, Leigh. For *me*. It doesn't matter what we want, what we planned for —you are *mine*."

Strong fingers wrap around my chin when he reaches me, forcing me to look up into his eyes. They are dark with carnal hunger and a possessiveness so strong it should make me turn around and run.

But it doesn't.

When he presses his mouth to mine, I part my lips and invite him in.

TEN

His triumphant growl vibrates through my very bones and into my abdomen. It makes my blood heat in a way no one's ever been able to do before him, and I mewl helplessly into his kiss.

If I wanted to, I could fight the burning desire rushing through my body for every second I stay in his embrace. I haven't Presented for him this time, and the need thrumming through my veins with every pulse of my heart is much more natural.

But, the longer I breathe in his wild pheromones and taste his hungry mouth, the less I feel any urge to stop.

I don't want to fight him—I want to give in.

His strong arms are around my body, dwarfing me with his huge size, his hands stroking up and down my sides, spurring my want for every passage. And his lips... so powerful, so hungry they seem to consume my very essence for each time our tongues flick against each other.

I am drowning in him, drowning in the powerful pull I feel from the very core of his being. And I can't get enough.

He lifts me up as if I weigh nothing, making me spread my knees for his hips. He grinds his still-covered cock against my soaking panties, rolls his hips into me, and I cry out wordlessly from the friction. He rubs over my hard little clit again and again, pushing me closer and closer to the edge of madness with every thrust.

"You drive me crazy," he growls against my ear, never slowing the steady roll of his hips. "I've thought of nothing but tasting you since we parted, and now that I have you, all I can think about is driving my cock into your tight little pussy. I'm going to fuck you so deep you'll forget we were ever separated. When I'm done with you you won't remember where you end and I begin—I will be as much a part of you as your own fucking arm."

"Uhng-uh," is all I manage in return, because just as he says it, he clamps his teeth shut around my shoulder, making my entire body shudder in violent pleasure.

It's weird—on some distant plane I do recognize that this should hurt, but all I feel is hot waves of desire and an unyielding urge to submit to him.

He must feel it too, because he growls low in his throat, a noise that makes my abdomen *clench,* and then moves his hands from my sides to my back, deftly undoing my zipper.

A gust of cool air against my chest and stomach as the dress falls off my chest and pools around my waist is quickly vanquished when he presses his body closer to mine, moving his mouth up along my neck with sharp little nips.

I arch my back in a desperate urge to feel his skin against mine, and claw uselessly at the tough fabric covering his body.

He chuckles against my neck in response, but lets me slide to my feet as he steps back. I stare at him with greedy eyes as he easily shrugs out of his top, baring a torso so ripped with bulging muscle every primitive part of my brain is practically drooling. He's ripped like a Greek god, and so absolutely huge he almost looks like he's something more than a human.

Alphas do have their perks. The errant thought flickers through my brain and is gone the next second, because he's gripped his pants in both hands and makes quick work of them and his boots. And then he's standing naked in front of me.

Completely and utterly *naked*, save the mask.

"*Ho*-ly hell."

It's not that I didn't know he was big below the belt as well—I did spend a week limping around the last time he was inside of me, after all. It's just that I never *saw* that part of him, and seeing it in the bright lights illuminating my apartment is something else entirely.

His cock looks almost as thick around as his wrist, and the flared head is nearly fist-sized.

"Er... I don't think... Maybe we shouldn't..." I make a vague gesture toward his crotch, unable to take my eyes of his hard length. Despite the heat pooling low in my belly, a sliver of sanity is desperately trying to fight its way through to stop this madness, because there's no way I can take that. There's just no way.

If the alpha knows what I'm trying to say, he doesn't care. With something halfway between a growl and a purr he looks me up and down as I stand before him in only my panties and bra, my dress pooling around my feet. And then, he moves.

My bra rips with a single, rough tug from the masked man, and then my panties follow, leaving me bared to his hungry gaze.

This time, the noise that escapes him is a full growl. He grabs me by the hips and lifts me up so I have no choice but to spread my legs for his waist. His obscene hardness presses up against my lower lips, my clit and my stomach as he pins me against the wall again, and I can't help but groan from the pressure against my most sensitive nerves.

When he bends his head for my pebbled nipple, I bury my face in the crook of his neck and cling on to his wide shoulders, moaning incoherently. Everything about him is heat and rough, urgent *need*, and as he works my clit with slow grinding and sucks greedily at my breast, it's increasingly difficult to remember why I didn't want this.

The alpha shifts his grip on my hips, momentarily removing the wonderful pressure against my clit, and suddenly I feel a hard presence nudging at my weeping entrance, searching for the way inside of me. *Oh, God, this is it.* He's so big my opening only kisses the crown of his head, but when he begins to push, the slick flesh yields.

"*Fuck!*" I throw my head back against the wall, nails digging into his shoulders in an effort to withstand the impossible stretch as my pussy struggles to open wide enough for him. He's going slow, but even as I begin to whimper and squirm to relieve the unbearable tension he doesn't give me any respite. Steadily, mercilessly he continues to drive his too-big cock into my fitfully spasming channel, and there's nothing I can do but try and take it.

"Relax, baby," he groans, his mouth finally coming off my nipple so he can nuzzle at my neck in an attempt at calming down my increasingly frantic whimpers. "Just relax and listen to your body. You know how to do this."

I shake my head—I don't know how to take him. The last time we did this, I'd just Presented for him, and even though I'm so wet my pussy's practically gushing slickness over his fat cock, I'm not high on hormones like I was the first time.

But even as I deny it, I can feel the call from the most primitive parts of my being. I want this—I *need* this, more than air, more than life itself. All I have to do is relax…

Moving on instinct alone I once again bury my nose against his neck and suck in greedy gulps of his scent. It fills my lungs with a heady rush of his mouthwatering pheromones, and it's as if something snaps into place deep in my core. The spasms ease, and my body stops fighting against the unrelenting penetration.

I'm rewarded with a hiss of pleasure from my alpha and a shock of excruciating sensation as he finally seats his entire head in me.

"*Ungh!*"

"Good girl." It's a strained gasp, rough with his obvious urge to forgo any gentleness and just ram in to the hilt, but despite the darkness flaming in his eyes he keeps the pace slow and steady.

I cling to him, panting and moaning as he fills me up with one long, smooth thrust that splits me open far beyond what I ever knew I could take. I was so high on hormones last time, it didn't fully register just how impossible a fit it is.

When he eventually hilts me, I'm nearly sobbing. There's some discomfort, but what has me shaking in the prison of his arms is the overwhelming sensation of finally being *complete*. Like all my life I've missed half of what makes me *me*, and now, speared on this stranger's cock and pinned to my own living room wall, I've finally found the missing piece.

A rush of endorphins flood my brain, and what little fight is left in my body melts away as every single muscle turns to liquid.

I have submitted to my alpha, like I was fated to do from the moment he laid eyes on me.

The wild, rutting beast of a man between my thighs feels my surrender. He roars his triumph out, like a barbarian claiming his victory.

And then, he thrusts.

"Oh! Oh! God! Fuck!" My sharp cries punctuate every time his cock drives into me, forcing my pussy wide with every hard thrust. He's no longer gentle, and I dig my nails deep into his shoulders in a desperate attempt at rooting myself to reality as he pounds me.

I can feel every bump and every vein on his brutal cock rubbing against my aching channel, and each time the thick rim of his broad head grinds against my G-spot I nearly black out. It's excruciating, and it's ecstasy in its purest form.

When he presses a thumb to my stiff little clit without ever letting up on the rough pounding, my orgasm is instantaneous.

I squeal and throw my head back against the wall as every muscle in my body tenses to the point of snapping.

Even my poor pussy tries to contract, but he's forcing me so wide all it can do is flutter desperately around him as my climax roars through me for what feels like several minutes.

I'm vaguely aware that he slows to a stop while I thrash on his cock like a woman possessed, and vaguely aware of his hoarse grunts of appreciation as I'm forced to milk his hard length, but only when I finally come down do my senses slowly return.

"Wow." My voice is raspy and raw from screaming, and it hitches in my throat when my alpha immediately begins fucking me again, as if I didn't just come for all I'm worth.

The lewd squelches from my pussy every time he

bottoms out in my still-quivering sheath leave no doubt to how fully he just conquered me—but he's nowhere near done with me.

I rest my forehead on his shoulder and wrap my arms around his neck, relishing in the strength of his body. Being astride him like this makes me feel both infinitely weak and at the same time, like the most powerful being in the whole world. He's so strong, dwarfing me in every aspect, but his hoarse grunts of pleasure as he takes me leaves no doubt that right now, he would rather die than be separated from me. I am the one this powerful alpha has chosen—I am the only one strong enough to ride his brutal cock.

My feverish contemplations come to a full stop when my lover once again presses his thumb to my sensitive clit and begins to rub it in rhythm with his hard thrusts.

"*Oh! N-ngh!*" I frantically push at his massive shoulders and try to drag his hand away from my tormented flesh. "It's too soon, I can't! It's too much!"

Every nerve in my abused little nub screams from hyper stimulation, causing my poor pussy to contract around his thick meat once again. The stimulation is way too much, way too soon after my orgasm and I thrash to escape his touch. But there is no escaping my alpha, not now, not ever, and soon my wails change pitch as I crash over the edge again. *Hard.*

This time, I do sob as I slouch in his arms, too spent to even complain about the pleasure he just forced me to endure.

He nuzzles at my neck, making soothing noises deep in his throat as he gently slips out of my sodden folds and carries me through my apartment. When he puts me down on a soft surface, I realize he's brought me to my bedroom.

He lays us both down on top of the sheets and wraps me up in his strong arms until I finally stop crying.

"You're okay," he whispers against my hair. "You're safe."

Despite the roughness of his voice, his words and his embrace soothes me better than any glass of wine ever has in the past. I look up into his eyes and see them hooded with the same unquenchable lust as before, and I realize that we're not done—he's just allowing me a small break. Something I should probably be thankful for, judging by the firm, pulsing pressure resting against my stomach.

"Is it always this rough?" I croak. My throat hurts from all the screaming, and I swallow thickly in an effort to relieve some of the aching.

"Yes." He places a kiss on my swollen lips and gets up, untangling himself from me. "You will get used to it."

I'm pretty sure he's right, I dazedly agree while I watch him leave the bedroom. His ass flexes mesmerizingly as he walks, and despite the wrecked state of my mind and pussy I feel a simmering heat brewing down low in my abdomen. I don't know if it's just the sight of his ridiculously powerful body, or if it's his still unsated pheromones filling the air, but I want him again.

God help me, I want him.

He returns with a glass of water, and when I struggle to sit up he pulls me into a seated position and wraps an arm around me so I don't have to keep myself upright while I drink.

We sit in silence while I empty the contents of the glass one careful sip at a time. When I'm done he lifts a hand to my face and wipes a drop of water from my lip.

"Done?"

I know what he's asking—if I'm ready for more. Not that he'd ever say it outright, I realize. He's my alpha—he doesn't ask for sex, he demands. But still, he ensures my willingness, and it's oddly endearing. Something I used to take for granted in lovers now seems like a kindness, and if I was completely with it I'd probably hate myself for submitting to alpha norms so easily.

But I'm high on endorphins and his delicious scent, and the simple question makes my heart flutter.

He cares that I'm happy. He cares about me.

"Yes."

The masked man gently takes the glass from me and puts it on the bedside table before he wraps both hands around my face and dips his lips to mine. The kiss is languid and soft at first, like a soothing balm to my frayed nerves.

The heat down low grows for every swipe of his tongue against mine, and when he pushes me back down on the bed I follow willingly. Soon, his hand brushes down my stomach to my legs, delving into the slick folds with ease.

I mewl in half-protest when he brushes over my clit, but he doesn't torment the still-aching nub further. Instead, he pushes a finger into my swollen opening and gently thrusts in and out a few times, giving me a lazy smirk.

"Much better. You're not so damn tight now."

"And whose fault is that?" My attempt at being snarky dies somewhat to my breathless tone and my hips slowly rocking up to meet his finger.

"Mine." It's a low, rich growl, and I know he takes pride in having conquered my pussy so completely. Without preamble he pulls back, grabs me by the hips and flips me onto my stomach.

I huff when I land face-down on the mattress, and grunt when he drags me onto my hands and knees. The bed sinks under his weight as he kneels behind me.

"Beautiful," he growls. "I love you like this—on your knees, with your pussy gaping open for me. So defenseless. All *mine.*"

I shiver at his words, and again when he brushes his palm over the length of my swollen sex. Then the now familiar pressure of his broad head catches in the mouth of my pussy, and I bite my lip to prepare for the inevitable.

This time, he spears me in one swift motion, bottoming out as he grabs my hips to stop my automatic surge forward.

I whimper as my sore channel is spread open to the core again, but it's easier this time. Hardly painful at all, save for the swollen walls of my oversexed pussy. And the feeling of having him inside of me again... I moan with completion, and then again with want as he pulls back, only to slam forward once more.

His pace is rough from the start this time, his heavy balls slapping a fast rhythm against my flesh.

I thrash on the bed in front of him, lost in the pleasure of finally being taken like every instinct in my body knows he's been needing from the very start—on my hands and knees with this wild beast of a man behind me, fucking me ruthlessly.

Underneath him, I let myself go completely. There's nothing but him and me now, nothing but his impossibly big cock pounding inside of me like he can never get enough. I thrash and I scream like a woman possessed, begging, pleading, demanding for every gasped breath as I take him over and over and over again. I cuss him for fucking me even as I cry out in pleasure, I cuss him for not coming to me sooner, and when he grinds against my G-spot particularly viciously, I try to twist around and scratch at him in retaliation.

That's when his teeth clamp shut around the back of my neck.

Instantly, I go limp underneath him. My arms give out as he triggers the sensitive receptors at my nape, and I whimper in confusion and surrender. My brain hazes over as a new rush of endorphins flood through me. My lax muscles try to let me flatten against the bed, but he won't let me. He keeps my ass in the air even as my face presses against the bedding, continuing his brutal fucking despite his teeth still being locked around my slim neck. His growl is unwavering, commanding.

And then, I twist my neck around.

I don't know why I do it—it's an instinctive movement that comes from the deepest parts of my primal self, but when his teeth are wrested free and then graze over a new spot, my body is suddenly filled with an electric current of excitement.

It feels like nothing I've ever felt before, and my panted moan is entirely involuntary.

My alpha stiffens behind me, his movements coming to a complete halt. For three full seconds we are like frozen in time.

Then, he bites down.

Hard.

I whimper as pain lances through me, but it hurts so *good* and I don't want him to stop.

His growl is different now, though I can't pinpoint what's changed. When he begins to fuck me again, I stop caring.

"Harder!" I plead into the mattress. I don't know if I mean his cock or his teeth, but I get both.

I yowl as he resumes his pounding of my defenseless pussy with an aggression that rivals anything he's given me before, but his teeth at the back of my neck keep me in place despite the vicious assault on my tender sex.

Only when something hard and bulgy begins to swell at the very bottom of his cock does he release my neck with a snarl, digging his fingers into my hips to ensure I stay put.

He's about to knot.

If it wasn't for the endorphins from his bite still lingering in my blood I might have struggled, but I don't have any fight left in my body. All I can do is grip the sheets and cry as he forces the still-swelling knot into my gaping pussy with every thrust.

Soon, it begins to catch on my already tormented opening, making him grunt with effort every time he pops it in or out of me. It sends shock waves of raw pleasure laced with dull throbs of pain to the very stem of my brain, and soon I'm babbling pleas at him to end it.

When he finally does, I suddenly remember with painful clarity why I was so scared of taking his knot again in the first place.

With one final roar, the masked alpha grabs my hips tightly and forces me back against him at the same time as his hips surge forward. The nearly full-sized knot catches against my splayed lips for two long, agonizing seconds—and then snaps inside with a lewd *pop*.

I can't even scream. My mouth is open in a silent wail, my fingers clawing long tears into the mattress beneath me. I am so full I can't contain it, so completely conquered it feels like the rapid heartbeat threatening to burst through my chest is his instead of my own. It's like heaven and hell in one, and I'm sure I'm losing what's left of my shattered mind.

Two fingers press hard against my clit, rubbing it roughly, and I *break*.

Everything is darkness.

I COME to to the sensation of utter and complete calm.

A deep rumbling sound vibrates through my back and penetrates into my very bones. It's the most beautiful sound I've ever heard, and some far-away part of my mind recognizes it.

I'm wrapped up in strong arms and pressed against a warmth that can only be the alpha's chest.

My alpha's chest.

He's purring for me, and I'm pretty sure I can detect a smugly satisfied note to it.

His one hand is on my stomach, rubbing the place where I can still feel his knot is locked inside of me.

"You said it wouldn't hurt this time." I should probably be furious with him for what he's just done to me, but I'm not. Everything inside of me is peace and pleasure. He was right—it doesn't matter what we thought we wanted before. Now, there is only this. Only *us*.

"I said it'd be much more pleasurable this time. Was I wrong?" Yup, he's definitely smug.

"Bastard," I grumble.

Only his soft chuckle answers me, and soon, his purring lulls me back to sleep, tied to him by my swollen pussy and content to the very core of my being.

ELEVEN

I lie awake in that half-state between dream and reality for a while.

It takes me a long time to identify the source of the glorious warmth wrapping around my body as a man's body, but when I do, the delicious ache deep inside makes sense.

I smile without opening my eyes and take a deep breath laced with the tang of stale sex and man. It smells like safety and *home,* and I twist around to bury my nose in its source.

The man by my side growls sleepily in response to my movement, and iron bands wrap tighter around my body, pulling me closer. As if he wants to ensure I don't leave his side.

Nothing could be farther from my mind. I've never felt this good, this safe, in my entire life, and I'm in no hurry to end it.

It must be at least half an hour later before consciousness finally brushes away the lingering sense of dreamy bliss.

Sleepily, I open my eyes and am immediately greeted with the unpleasant reminder that I forgot to remove my makeup last night. My eyelashes stick together like glue, and there's a cakey feeling clogging my skin from whatever is leftover from my foundation. *Yuck.*

I rub at my eyes in an attempt at unsticking my lashes, and am rewarded with another growl from my bed partner. A large hand rounds on my right breast in a possessive gesture that makes the night's events come back to me all at once and in high-definition.

Shit.

The intruder.

...Who I let fuck me silly right after he told me I was *his*.

Slowly, I force my eyelashes apart and look at the man —the alpha—I've shared my bed with, despite the fact that I still don't know who he is.

His mask is still in place, but he looks like he's fast asleep, despite the growled warning for me to stay put. Must have been another *alpha instinct*—ensuring the woman he sees as his doesn't stray too far while he's asleep.

Dammit.

How have I let myself fall into the kind of trap I always swore I was too smart for? I've always rolled my eyes at the women hanging off their alpha's arm like obedient little puppets, believing them to be too pathetic and weak-willed to stand up for themselves. And here I am, still sore between the legs from being knotted like a whore, and even though I should be disgusted with myself for what I've allowed him to do—and *say*—I can't deny the warm feeling of finally being *complete* in my stupid chest.

Gently, I brush my fingertips over the back of my neck where he bit me. He didn't break the skin, but there is a sore reminder that makes me wince at the slightest touch. I'm undoubtedly sporting teeth-shaped bruises.

I vaguely recall something from those biology lessons back in high school, about how alphas mark their mates. Biting their necks so a scar forms, as a symbol of their eternal bond.

A shudder travels through me at the thought of how close I was to carrying his mark on me for life, but it's not of horror like it should be.

Yearning.

I am so fucked.

I stare at the still-sleeping alpha. His soft lips and strong jaw are fully relaxed, and he looks almost innocent. Only the black mask remains as a constant reminder of what kind of man he truly is. A thug. A criminal, who hides his identity even from the woman he claims belongs to him.

Well, if he thinks he can come into my home and mount me like a feral beast without even showing me his face, he's wrong.

I am careful not to disturb him again as I let my fingertips edge closer to his black mask. As gently as I can, I peel the high-tech fabric up, exposing high cheekbone, pale skin and...

For the longest moment, all I can do is stare at the sleeping man who has deceived me so gruesomely.

Peter Leod doesn't stir at the hiss of air when I finally realize I've been holding my breath.

With the renewed flow of oxygen comes a rush of anger so intense it manages to burn away the sated feeling of contentment.

"You have *got* to be kidding me!"

Gray eyes flutter open at my sharp outburst, the pupils only momentarily unfocused before he quickly scans the room. Looking for a threat, like the stereotypical alpha he is.

I prod his bare chest with a finger to regain his attention. Hard. "Peter *freakin'* Leod? Mister *'Oh, alphas need to rein in their instincts to not oppress others'*. The same man who not twenty-four hours ago told me he had nothing to do with my Cinderella-invite to the masquerade, and yet here you are, *in my bed,* because you demanded *payment* for that stupid ticket!"

His fingers goes to his uncovered face, tracing the upturned edge of the mask. A deep sigh escapes him, and he pushes it off completely.

"You shouldn't have done that."

"No? Why not, are you going to dump me in the river now? Imagine what would happen if the public realized you got your rocks off on going all alpha on some lowly reporter girl. Your precious image would be ruined!"

Okay, so maybe it's not the smartest thing to antagonize the powerful alpha like that, but I'm too pissed to care. For reasons I can't even pinpoint I feel so betrayed it's all I can do not to start swinging at him.

"It's not like that," Leod says. He sits up and tries to reach for me, but I'm having none of it.

I push myself away from him, folding my arms over my naked breasts. "No, then what's it like, Peter? Can I call you Peter now? You did just spend half the night with your cock inside of me. I'd like to think I'm on a first name basis with the high-fliers who roll into my bed whenever they damn well please. The ones I actually know the identity of, of course."

"It's just until after the election. I was going to court you the proper way once it no longer matters who I'm seen with. I didn't want the complication of you knowing my identity, and risking others finding out."

"Excuse me?" I hiss. "I might not be some upper class tart, but I'm not the one who's dropping bodies left, right and center. If anyone has any reason to hide this affair, it's *me!*"

"That's not what I meant." Leod scrubs his face with both hands before he looks at me again. There's a hint of the dark possessiveness from last night in his gaze again, but I'm far too livid to respond to it. "I'm not able to think when I'm around you, Leigh. Ever since you Presented for me during that damn press conference, I've not been able to get you out of my head. I think about you every waking second of every day, and I dream about you every fucking night! I can't be around you when I'm trying to win the election, because you make me go primal in the worst of ways."

"I didn't Present for *you!* There was a room full of damn alphas, and—"

"You Presented for *me,*" he interrupts, with more than a hint of a growl in his voice. "I saw you—I *felt* you. You Presented for me, no one else, and don't *ever* think differently."

"That's it!" I scramble to my feet and halfway fall out of bed, pointing one finger at the door. I'm so pissed I'm shaking, and I don't even care that I'm giving him a full view of my naked body. It's not like he hasn't seen every part of it already. "I'm not putting up with this high-handed alpha bullshit for one more moment, you got it? You don't want people to know you're just like every other alpha out there, then you get the hell out of my bed! I'm not putting up with your hypocritical crap, when you've just spent the night forcing every damn alpha stereotype on me, making me bend to your will every step of the way. You're a liar and a fraud, and I want nothing more to do with you! You hear me? *Nothing!* Now get the *hell* out of my home!"

For the longest moment he just sits there, staring at me with dark anger, and I'm sure he's going to refuse. But then, he gets up. With measured movements he picks his clothes that lay scattered on the floor up and pulls them on, leaving only the mask behind.

Giving me one final, dark look, he walks to the hallway and out the front door. Closing it behind him without another word.

IT'S NOT until after I've had a shower that my anger has dissipated enough to let the flood of other, more complex emotions make my furious resolve whither and die, leaving me feeling hollow inside.

Even in my fury with Leod's hypocrisy, I never truly expected him to leave. Deep down, I thought he meant the things he said while we were intimate. That I belonged to him, that he'd never let me out of his sight…

And now, in the harsh light of morning, it's abundantly obvious that that's not the case. After all that alpha posturing, it turns out his words were nothing but just that —empty promises spoken in the heat of the moment.

And why do I even care? Angrily, I finish drying my hair and pull my clothes on. It's not like I want a boyfriend, and especially not an overbearing alpha who thinks he can boss me around like he pleases.

So why does the knowledge that the man who's little more than a stranger to me didn't stick around make me feel so empty?

A firm knock on my front door makes my thoughts

come to an abrupt halt, and I silently curse the way my heart leaps with anticipation.

Even if he's come back to apologize, it doesn't change the fact of who and what he is. I tell myself this as I make my way to the front door, but it does nothing to quell the idiotic hope blooming in my chest. *Stupid alpha.*

I open the door with an irritated huff, mouth open and ready to give my unplanned lover another piece of my mind.

But the two men outside aren't Leod.

I have a vague flicker of recognition before one of them steps through the door and presses a moist cloth to my mouth, grabbing my hair with his free hand so I can't draw back.

A pungent stench fills my lungs as I try to scream, and then darkness takes me.

TWELVE

The first thing I notice as my consciousness returns is that I can't move.

My vision takes forever to focus when I finally manage to drag my eyelids open, so all I can see for the first few minutes are blurred outlines of what looks like dark wood furniture and walls in a hideous peach tone.

I pull on my arms again, harder this time, only to wince as a sharp pain in my wrists shoots up through my biceps.

"No need to struggle just yet, girl," a deep voice rumbles from somewhere behind me.

I squeak at the unexpected speech and try to jerk around to see who's there with me, but all I manage to do is cause myself more pain. I blink rapidly, desperate to regain my sight when a dark figure walks into my field of vision, and finally my eyesight slowly returns. The blurred shape turns sharper, and I recognize one of the two men who were outside my apartment when...

Sonuva*bitch!* They *kidnapped* me!

"Where am I?" I demand in a tone that's more raspy and frightened-sounding than I was aiming for.

"Doesn't matter," the alpha says. He leans against the bureau in front of me, folding his arms across his wide chest as he looks down at me.

"Why did you kidnap me?" I try to fight back the panic swelling in my chest as I stare up at him. I know him from somewhere, but I just can't put my finger on it. "I don't have any money."

An amused noise escapes his throat. "Don't care about your money, bitch. You're here as bait. And you best start praying that the beast we're trying to capture cares enough about you to come running, or you'll end up as fish food."

What? This makes no sense. I don't have any powerful frien—

I gape up at him when who he means hits me like a brick. "Leod? You think *Leod* will come for me?"

My kidnapper smirks. "We can hope, eh?"

"That's insane," I protest. "I'm no one to him!"

"Really, now?" He grabs a folded-up newspaper from the bureau and throws it on my lap. ""Cause he spent an awful long time in your apartment last night. And then this hit the streets this morning. This *is* the newspaper you work for, isn't it? Seems to me he cares enough about you to sell out all his colleagues for some time between your thighs, so I'm gonna wager he also cares enough to try and stop you from getting murdered."

I stare mutely at the paper in my lap. It's folded in half, but I can easily read the headline:

Masquerade Orgy: Mattenburg's Elite Hides Sex Auction

Underneath is a picture that looks like a still from the video I shot. Even though no genitals are on display, it's unmistakably a masked alpha balls-deep inside a screaming woman. In the background you can make out the naked and chained men and women waiting on the auction block, and the backdrop is very clearly from inside Town Hall.

"I... I don't have anything to do with that," I say, and despite the terror making my gut clench, I'm proud of how steady my voice sounds. "And Leod... it was just a one-night stand. Do you kidnap all the women he spends a night with?"

"You better hope you were more than a one-night stand to him." He says it with a casual shrug, as if he's not bothered one way or the other, and that one movement finally makes the seriousness of my situation set in. This man really, truly does not value my life as anything more than a bargaining chip. If I prove to be a bad gamble, he'll kill me without a second thought.

If Leod doesn't show up, I'm as good as dead.

"What do you want from him?" I rasp. "To kill him?"

"Don't be silly," the alpha says, sparing me a contemptuous look. "His death would cause a public outcry."

"Then what?"

Another cold smirk. "His reputation, of course. If he wants to save your life, come tonight, there won't be a single person left in this city who'll still believe in his Liberal bullshit."

My heart sinks, and it's not until complete hopelessness takes me that I realize some small, hidden part of me was still hoping he'd come for me. But not now—not when it's his reputation on the line. Wasn't that why he left me in the first place? Because he didn't want to risk his precious reputation just by being seen with me? Whatever this guy has planned, it's bound to be much, much worse than that.

No, when it comes to choosing between me and his career, he's already made his choice. And I didn't come out on top.

I've just allowed myself to sink into complete misery when muted commotion draws both mine and my kidnapper's attention. He looks above my shoulder where the sounds are coming from, a faint smile pulling on his lips. I strain to look as well, but can't twist my neck far enough.

The sound of a door being unlocked makes me realize what the alpha is looking for even before an angry voice rings through the room.

"I swear, if you've so much as *touched* her, I'll rip your dick off!"

Leod.

He's come!

"Relax, no one's put their knot in your little girlfriend.

Look, there she is, safe and sound. Just waiting to be rescued." The other, new voice is dripping with sarcasm, but the furious snarl that rips through the room doesn't belong to him. It belongs to Leod, and the threat of absolute murder vibrating through it makes even my hair stand on end. Oh, boy. He's *pissed*.

A large figure comes into my field of vision, followed by big hands wrapping gently around my face. Leod stares down at me, concern and fury etched into his prominent features.

"Leigh? Are you all right?"

"Y-yeah, I'm okay," I croak. Despite the seriousness of the situation, I can't fight the ridiculous bubbles of happiness threatening to explode out of my chest at the sight of him.

He really came for me.

Quickly, he bends to untie first my wrists from behind the chair I'm seated on, and then my ankles. But when he offers his hand to lift me to my feet, my kidnapper by the bureau pulls a gun out and points it at me.

"You just leave the girl right where she is, Leod. It's time for us to have a grown-up chat."

Leod bares his teeth in a growl. "You better move that fucking thing away from her before I shove it up your ass and pull the trigger."

The other alpha gives him a small smile and points the weapon toward the floor instead.

Leod's posture relaxes a fraction of an inch, but I don't miss how he takes a half-step to the side, shielding me from the man still holding the gun. "Right. Let's talk. What does Bremen want, then? Let me guess—for me to withdraw myself from the election?"

I stare at his back. Bremen? The Lord Mayor's behind this? I don't know why I didn't figure that out from the start—he's Leod's fiercest competitor, and he's got a reputation as being completely merciless. It suddenly dawns on me where I've seen my kidnapper before—he was the alpha who checked my ticket when I arrived at the masquerade. Yeah, they work for Bremen, all right.

"He's predictable, the old goat, isn't he?" the other kidnapper, who's still somewhere behind me, says in an easy tone. "You should have seen his face when we told him about the girl you snuck off to see. Practically lit up like a Christmas tree."

"I'm not entirely sure why he thinks kidnapping a random booty call will help him in any way," Leod says coolly, and even though I know he's being crass to gain the upper hand, it still stings to hear him call me that.

Angry with myself, I bite my lip to get my head back on straight. Now is *so* not the time to start acting like I'm starring in a stereotypical chick flick. There's not exactly time to wallow in self-pity and *emotions-that-have-no-business-being-there-in-the-first-place* when two men with a gun have you locked up and at their mercy.

"A booty call?" the gun-wielding alpha snorts. "Apparently she's a bit more than that, or you wouldn't have showed in the first place. Don't even try and pretend you're any kind of hero—if she was truly just a knot-warmer, you'd have let her die without a second thought."

"And look at that interesting mark the little twat has on the back of her neck," the man behind me drawls, letting a single finger brush along my nape so the hair is pushed aside. I flinch when he touches the bruise Leod gave me just before he knotted me.

Leod snarls and spins around with absolute fury in his eyes. "Get your hand off her!"

The two kidnappers might be the ones in charge, but the guy behind me quickly removes his fingers from my skin at the unmistakable promise of *pain* ringing through Leod's command.

"Looks an awful lot like someone was contemplating on claiming himself a mate," the alpha with the gun says, his tone almost a singsong taunt.

Leod's face is still contorted in anger as he glares at the man behind me, and I expect for him to deny it. But then his expression falls and his shoulders slump.

"Fine. Bremen gets his way. If you let us go now, we should be able to make the six o'clock news. I'll announce my withdrawal then."

"Not so fast," the alpha behind me says, and I can hear the smirk in his voice. It sends goosebumps of uneasiness down my back. "You don't really think he's letting you off the hook that easy?"

"I'm sure you can understand he'll want an insurance policy," the man with the gun says. "We can't have you popping back up in the political picture come the next election. No, we need to be absolutely sure that when you leave this room, your reputation is so wrecked you'll never be able to come back from it."

"Spit it out," Leod grits between clenched teeth as he looks from one kidnapper to the other. "What does he want me to do?"

The alpha in front of us pulls out his cell phone and holds it up in front of Leod with a wry smirk. "You. In front of the camera. Fucking the ever living shit out of this poor girl."

THIRTEEN

"Are you out of your goddamn mind?" Leod sounds about as livid as I feel numb with shock. None of us saw *that* coming, that's for sure. "He wants a fucking *porn tape?*"

"Not exactly." The smirk slides off the kidnapper's face, leaving ice-cold stone in its wake. "What he *wants* is for the entire city to see what a despicable, dangerous alpha you are. He wants to prove to the city that you're in denial about your true nature, and that all your Liberal propaganda is nothing more than a thin veneer hiding the exact kind of brutality all those little beta males and their womenfolk are so terrified of.

"So what *I* need is for you to strip naked, rip the clothes off the girl, and make her take your cock until she howls. And be rough about it, because for you both to leave this room alive, the public needs to see a video of their favorite Liberal scum raping the crap out of a helpless woman crying for mercy."

For five long seconds there is complete silence in the room, save for my ragged breathing. This can't be real. It just *can't* be.

"If you think for one second I'll ever lay a hand on my own mate, let alone brutalize her for the entire city to gawk at, you're going to be sorely disappointed." Leod's voice is oddly calm—gentle even. But there's no mistaking the burning steel in his eyes as he glares down first one, and then the other kidnapper.

I blink, momentarily distracted from the insane situation. Did he just... did he just call me his... *mate?*

"I don't think I will," the kidnapper says. "See, if you don't do it, things are going to look very, *very* grim for poor Leigh here. How much do you want us to hurt her before you lose your pride? Why not save the poor girl some pain and just get on with it, before we have to prove to you just how serious we are?"

"If you hurt her, I will *end* you." The threatening growl is back in Leod's voice.

"I'm the one with the gun, Leod. You overstep, and she dies."

"You're not nearly fast enough to pull that trigger twice before I rip out your fucking throat!" I've never seen Leod like this before—and I doubt anyone else has, either. His entire form is shaking from barely leashed rage, his fists clenched so hard his knuckles are white. The other guy might be the one with the gun, but if I were him, I'd be needing a new pair of pants right about now.

As I look up at him, I realize I'm no longer scared.

Not really. For whatever dumb—and undoubtedly ovary-connected—reason, every instinct in my body trusts that as long as he's here, everything's going to be okay.

And if all these people want in return for letting us go unharmed is for us to have sex, well...

"I'll do it."

The tension in the room shifts as all three alphas stare down at me, Leod with incredulity in his gray eyes.

"What?"

"I'll do it. I like having sex with you. What does it matter if they film it?"

A pained grimace cuts across his handsome face. "I don't want to hurt you."

An involuntary flicker of amusement makes me snort, despite the seriousness of the situation. The two times we've been together so far haven't exactly been marked by gentleness, and *now* he's concerned about causing me pain?

"Listen to the girl, Leod," the man behind me says. "You can prep her, if you prefer, 'slong as you make it look nice and rough for the camera."

Leod looks silently into my eyes for the longest moment, and I know he's searching for the truth in my gaze. He wants to be absolutely sure I'm okay with this.

I give a small nod and offer him a genuine, albeit somewhat strained, smile. As long as it's with him, I can do this.

"Fine." His voice rings through the room, authoritative and defeated at the same time. "But if she changes her mind, I'm stopping."

The guy with the gun ignores him. He waves his weapon at something behind me. "Get on the bed. We've got ropes—I want her tied up with her legs spread so we can get a good angle on the video."

Leod growls low in his throat in response, but doesn't argue. Once again he offers me his hand and pulls me to my feet, supporting my weight against his own, strong frame.

Only when he turns me around and walks the couple of feet to the shabby-looking twin-sized bed do I see the rest of the room they've held me in. It looks like a shoddy motel room, with stains on the carpet and walls. The dark brown blinds are closed, so I can't look out the window for any landmarks.

Leod helps me up on the bed, then pulls me into a kneeling position so he can capture my face between his large hands and I can't see anything but his face.

"Any time you want me to stop, you just say so, got it?"

I nod, and his lips descend on mine. Despite his obvious reluctance to submit to my captors, his mouth is hungry as he kisses me, and soon I feel the first lick of flames from deep inside. Even now, everything about him is heat and masculinity, and it speaks to the deepest parts of me on an entirely primal level.

When he pulls back, I'm panting.

"Get on with it, Leod," one of the kidnappers barks.

I flinch—I'd almost forgotten we weren't alone.

"Ignore them," Leod says, and by the roughness of his voice I can tell his desire is also rising, despite the situation. "It's just you and me."

I nod as he once again grasps my face between his large hands, and when he kisses me again, the knowledge of being watched fades swiftly to the background.

This time, he doesn't break away, and I only vaguely notice his skilled hands undressing me while our tongues intermingle. Only when a thumb brushes over my nipple do I realize everything above my waistline is bare.

When I pull back from his lips he dips his hands lower and unzips my jeans, but I'm more focused on his wide and equally bare torso. I reach out to let my hands slide along his ridiculously muscled chest, reveling in the rippling strength underneath my palms.

He shivers under my touch, and a low, appreciative growl rumbles out from his throat. A hard push and I'm on my back on the bed.

Leod follows, catching himself on his arms so he can rest above me without squashing me with his weight. There is fire in his eyes now, and it speaks to something down low in my abdomen.

He doesn't give me time to catch my bearings, and I moan when his teeth sink into my throat—not hard enough to hurt, but not gently, either. His tongue soon follows, and then his hand slides down my pants and inside my panties, and my moans quickly devolve into whimpers. He's circling my clit while kissing and nibbling at my throat, and soon I'm bucking underneath him for more.

It's so different than the two other times we've been together—while he's still demanding and rougher than guys I've been with before, he's taking his time to ready me like a normal lover would. It dawns on me, while I'm panting and squirming underneath the alpha, that this is probably what dating him would be like.

Just as I have that thought, he lifts his head from my throat and gazes down at me, and my breath catches in my throat at the look in his eyes. The heat's still there, and from the fierceness in his eyes it's obvious it's getting stronger, but there's something else in the gray depths, too. Something much gentler than anything I've seen from him before. It makes me reach up to touch his cheek, because right in this moment, we're not just an alpha and his conquered female. We're something much more than that, even though I struggle to put words to it.

Mates.

Goosebumps break out all over my body as I recall his own label from just moments ago. He called me his *mate*.

I don't know much about alpha traditions, but I do know that that term means a whole lot more than lover, or even girlfriend.

Leod breaks my breathless contemplations when he closes his eyes and turns his head so he can kiss my palm before his mouth returns to my body. But this time, he doesn't go for my throat.

I groan when he latches on to my right nipple and

flicks his tongue over the stiff bud once, twice, and sucks it into the hot cavern of his mouth while pinching my clit. *Hard.*

"Ohh, *fuck!*" I feel moisture soaking my panties and arch my back up for more. A few more moments of this and I feel an orgasm start to build.

"Yes, more," I moan, rolling my hips up against his fingers in waves. "Please, yes!"

"*Stop.*"

The command comes from behind us, and makes both of us freeze—me with a start, Leod with an angry growl.

"This is not a fucking romance novel. Bremen wants it *rough.*"

"He gonna come in here and give me fucking pointers, too?" Leod snarls over his shoulder, without moving his hand from my panties. "I'm getting her ready."

"She sounds plenty ready to me," the other guys says. "Get her goddamn pants off. We ain't asking twice."

The unmistakable sound of a gun cocking makes chills run down my spine—but much to my own astonishment, it's not from fear. Leod's ever-protective presence doesn't allow fear to creep into my mind, and instead, I find the knowledge that two armed thugs are directing us... inexplicably arousing.

Leod sits up and grabs the waistband of my jeans and panties. One rough pull later and I'm laid bare before him.

The look in his eyes as he takes me in once again pulls my attention away from our audience. There is a fiery, burning need in that stormy gaze of his, and it's solely focused on *me*.

"You're so fucking beautiful." It's a rough growl that goes straight to my clit. I whimper in response and open my thighs, presenting myself for him.

With another growl he falls down between my spread legs, grabs me by the thighs, and pulls me toward him. I squeak and grasp onto the cheap bedding for purchase just as he spreads my lower lips open and buries his mouth against my pussy.

The shock of pure, unadulterated pleasure when he licks up my inner lips and finds my clit makes me groan and arch up off the bed. He doesn't ease into it, and I wail under the merciless lashes of his tongue right against my most sensitive nerves.

"Fuck, *P-Peter! Ohh,* God!" I scream and I writhe, but he keeps me in place until every single nerve in my body is white-hot with agonizing pleasure and I think I'm going to die.

Only then does he stop flicking his tongue against my poor clit, instead wrapping his lips around it to give it one, two, three deep suckles.

I come like a woman possessed.

It's not like the times he's made me climax while he's been inside of me. I feel my pussy clutch helplessly at air in desperate search for something to milk as the explosion of pleasure sets every cell in my body on fire. It's a localized sensation, but *oh,* is it ever-powerful. And instead of bone-deep exhaustion, like when he's fucked me, I just feel elation.

He draws long, slow laps through my still-sensitive folds while I slowly come to, thankfully avoiding my clit.

It takes me a while to realize that the rumbling, humming sound currently filling the room comes from him. The sound of a pleased alpha.

I force myself up on my elbows and catch his gaze as he feels me moving. His eyes are no longer gray—they're pitch black, pupils blown with a hunger I've learned to recognize.

Slowly, Leod pulls back and sits up. He wipes his mouth with one hand, never breaking eye contact, and despite my recent orgasm I feel a flutter down low.

"Fist her."

The command shocks me out of my post-orgasm haze, and I rip my gaze from Leod's to the kidnappers at the end of the bed. One's got a phone aimed at us with the flash on. The other's got his cock in his hand.

"No!" I scramble to cover myself with the scratchy blanket on the bed, no longer wrapped up in the moment, but am caught by Leod's large hands as he clasps my upper arms.

"Shh, sweet," he says, but despite his soothing, rumbly tone pulling enticingly at my instincts to relax and trust that my alpha's in control, the kidnappers' command brings too terrifying images to my mind that I can't give in. I've heard of women being fisted before, but just the thought makes my pussy clench in horror. And Leod's got *big* hands.

Leod squeezes my arms gently, reassuring me with his presence. When our eyes meet again, he strokes his thumbs across my skin. "I won't. I promise."

"You fucking better," the guy with his cock out snarls. "I wanna see her take all five knuckles!"

"Ignore them," Leod says. His voice is still as calm and reassuring as if we were alone, but the edge of steel in it lets me know he's not going to bend on this. "It's just you and me here, darling. Just me worshiping your body. Okay?"

I nod slowly. As long as he looks at me like that, like I'm the only one in the whole world, it's easier to ignore our audience.

Leod takes my hand in his and places it against the crotch of his pants. The bulge there feels enormous, and I can't help but look down.

It's a miracle he hasn't burst his zipper yet, the way his cock is straining to be set free.

"I want you, Leigh. I want you more than I've ever wanted anything in my entire life."

There's something in his voice, something more than just sexual urgency, but when he places his hand against my pussy and presses his thumb in against my still-oversensitive clit, my focus scatters like leaves to the wind.

"Tell me you want me, too."

"I do," I rasp.

Leod moves his hand from mine where he's pressing it

against his groin and holds it out to his side, palm up. "Rope."

I keep my eyes on his until he pulls his hand back, displaying a length of nylon rope.

"On your stomach."

I obey, making sure not to look at the two other men in the room as I swivel around. Once I'm face-down in the sheets, Leod moves off the bed and walks to the headboard. Silently, he grasps my hands and pulls them up above my head. The rope scratches my skin as he secures it around my wrists, but it only adds to the tension building between us.

I have a vague notion that I shouldn't be the least bit okay with letting a man I hardly know tie me to a bed, not even taking our audience into consideration... but I am. He could—and has—taken me without any restraints in place before, his ample strength more than enough to ensure my compliance. But there's just something about the symbolism of giving up my control to him so completely that has me shivering with anticipation.

Leod secures my wrists to the headboard, and then moves to my feet. He pulls first my left ankle to the side, tying it securely to one of the legs, and then does the same with my right ankle, leaving me spread open and oh-so vulnerable.

The bed dips as he climbs between my legs, and I gasp softly when I feel his fingers brush over my outer pussy lips.

He doesn't stop there, though. Without pause he

spreads my lips and delves into my tight heat with two, big fingers. I'm so wet from my orgasm I take him without too much resistance, even though my pussy still has to stretch to accommodate him.

He pumps me slowly a couple of times, but just as it starts to feel good he withdraws again.

I whine at the loss—and then swallow hard when something rounded, hard and much bigger than his fingers press against my opening.

"You better make it rough, Leod, and you better give her the fucking knot," someone sneers from behind me, but I don't have time to think about it, because in the next second he forces the entire length of his huge cock inside of me in one, rough push.

The sound of his balls slapping against my flesh as he hilts me is drowned out by my agonized wail.

Fuck, he's so impossibly big! I thrash in my binds against the brutal penetration, but there is no give in the ropes. No matter how much I struggle there's nothing I can do to escape his hugeness stretching me excruciatingly wide.

Not that I'd want to, even if I could.

Every part of my desperately clutching pussy feels his presence, the veins running along his thick cock, and the pulse of his heart. I feel so utterly and completely *conquered*—and nothing has ever felt better.

That is, until he thrusts.

If I thought our first time was rough, it was only because I didn't know what true ferocity lay beneath the surface of the alpha who's claimed me as his. He fucks me so hard I have to grit my teeth not to bite my own tongue, his grueling length forcing me open to the core over and over and over again. The fast, wet slapping of his hips against my ass as my pussy smacks for him is only drowned out by the bed's violent creaking and my desperate screams.

How the other occupants of the motel don't come running I have no idea, because for anyone hearing me, I know it must seem like I am truly being raped. I can't hold back the tears, nor stop myself from fighting against the ropes holding me down as I am fucked so brutally I can't contain it.

But nothing could be farther from the truth.

My alpha's hands are on my hips, my back, my shoulders, grabbing me, holding me so tightly I know he'll never let me go. His breath comes in harsh pants, punctuated by groans of pleasure when my battered pussy takes him to the hilt, along with the occasional, growled, *"Fuck! Yes! Take it!"*

I know with certainty that he's never taken a woman like he's taking me now, and in every touch of his body against mine I can *feel* the bone-deep pleasure he gets every time my pussy is forced to swallow him to the root. It enhances my own, physical ecstasy tenfold, and it takes me less than two minutes to start climbing toward my first peak.

He feels me clutching tighter around him, and without pausing his brutal pace, he changes the angle of his thrusts. When his cock's fat mushroom head drives directly into my G-spot, I see stars.

"Fuck! God! Shit! Fuck!" I nearly dislocate a shoulder in my fight against the ropes as he drills the spongy spot on my frontal walls with all the power of his strong body, but he's having none of it. A large hand between my shoulder blades presses me into the mattress hard enough to stop my fighting, and then there's nothing I can do but take it.

I come so hard I nearly pass out.

The white-hot crackling of my climax shoots through my body not like a wave, but an explosion of release. I scream until my voice gives out, rocking back against the hard cock lodged inside me all the way to my cervix. He's mercifully stopped the maddening thrusts while my pussy clamps down like a vise around him, letting me ride out the powerful orgasm at my own pace.

Only when my pussy finally stops spasming some minutes later and I fall down flat on my stomach, completely spent, does he continue.

I whimper in protest, and then wail when he quickly picks up the pace until he's riding me as viciously as before, but there's no more mercy to be found.

I come five more times from his ruthless pummeling of my conquered sheath, until I finally have no more left to give. I lay sprawled underneath the huge alpha's rutting body, taking his cock with only a soft whimper until finally, I start to feel the increasing stretch in the bottom part of my entrance that signifies his knot beginning to form.

He fucks me with the full length of his shaft until the swelling begins to catch against my opening. When he finally slows down, grinding the knot against my stretched pussy lips, I grit my teeth, because I know what's coming.

His hand returns to my spine, but this time it feels more like a comforting touch than insurance that I'll stay put.

And then, it comes.

Despite my gritted teeth I cry out as his knot pushes through my resisting entrance, nestling in right behind my stretched lips. He continues to take me with short, quick jabs as his knot swells inside of me, and soon my pussy flutters in desperation as he grinds into my already depleted G-spot.

"One more, baby," he growls above me, his voice hoarse and raw from sex. "Give me one more."

I have no choice but to obey.

When his knot finally reaches its full size, my pussy locks every muscle in my violated core down tight around it, and I come with a hoarse sob from the unrelenting pressure.

Leod roars out above me, clasping both hands around my hips, and finally I feel the warm rush of his semen pulsing rapidly against my cervix as he comes.

We stay like that for several minutes, unmoving save for the jerks of his cock as he unloads his seed deep inside of me, both of us gasping for air.

After some time, he wraps his strong arms underneath- and around me and buries his face in the crook of my neck. It's such a sweet gesture, so completely at odds with the rough fucking he's just given me, that I can't help but smile into the scratchy sheets. *My alpha.*

"Thanks for the show." The condescending voice from behind us makes both of us jerk—sometime during the past half hour, we've both forgotten we weren't alone in the room.

Above me, Leod rips his head around with a *snarl* like nothing I've ever heard before. He sounds like a terrifying predator about to *maim*.

"Oh, give it a rest. You're knotted so thoroughly to that pussy I'd be surprised if you'll be able to get off her within the next hour." One of the kidnappers, the one who videotaped us, comes into my field of vision when he steps around to the side of the bed. "I can see why you're fond of this one—she took that fucking like a champ. Too bad for you the public won't see anything but a poor girl getting raped within an inch of her life."

Leod snarls again, and I feel a sharp tug from between my legs when he lunges at the other alpha. My broken cry of distress makes him pull back before he can reach the smug male, but his threatening growl is never-wavering. He hunches above me in a protective pose, shielding my body from the kidnappers as much as he can while we're still tied.

"All right, I guess we're all done, then," the other alpha says. "Be sure to turn on the news tonight so you can see what it looks like to literally fuck your political career to smithereens."

Leod's growl doesn't stop until the motel door closes behind the two thugs. Then, slowly, the rumbling noise from his chest changes to a deep, soothing purr.

Exhausted, I close my eyes and relax underneath my alpha.

FOURTEEN

The city is in uproar.

I can't hear the people on the streets, but it's easy to see. They're gathering in large groups instead of making their way home from work along the pavement, and many are waving the same front page photo from the masquerade in the air that my kidnapper showed me earlier.

I look at them out the tinted windows of Leod's car as his driver slowly makes his way through the congested traffic and wonder how much worse it'll get when they see the video Bremen's men just shot.

The silent alpha by my side called the driver to pick us up at the motel once his knot went down enough to break the coital tie, and he didn't so much as blink at the seedy location, the disheveled woman in his employer's arms as Leod carried me to the car, or the stench of sex that still fills the car now, a good forty-five minutes after we left the motel. I guess being a politician's driver quickly teaches you not to ask questions.

I glance at Leod—*Peter*—out the corner of my eye. He hasn't said a word to me since he untied me from the bed, and if there ever was an embodiment of the term *broody,* it would definitely be him. His forehead is locked in a permanent frown and his normally so icy gray eyes are dark, his expression withdrawn.

Not that I can really blame him. He's just sacrificed his entire career by letting his enemy get the upper hand.

I have a vague sensation that I should feel guilty—he had to let go of all his political ambitions to save my life, after all. But I just... don't. I don't even feel angry or scared—or violated—after what we just had to do. No, I feel oddly... elated. Content. Like something in the core of my being has slid into place, and I'm finally right where I need to be.

Damn hormones.

Even as I think it, I can't even muster up any form of real annoyance. I can't help the smile threatening to spread across my face as I look at my broody alpha.

He came for me.

He sacrificed everything for me.

No one's ever cared enough about me to do anything remotely similar, not even my own parents. It's always been me against the world, having to fight for everything I've gotten in life. And now... now, I'm no longer alone.

Peter stirs as I slide my hand into his, his gaze flicking

to my face. He's got the same expression of regret and concern as he's had since he knotted me, clearly certain he's violated me despite how many times I told him I wanted it.

I give him a small smile and squeeze his hand, not wanting to get into what happened in front of his driver. He might be used to seeing a bit of everything, but I'm not exactly used to discussing something as private as what Peter and I shared today in front of an audience. Which is kind of ironic, given that a video recording of it is about to be spread across the entire city.

Peter doesn't say anything, either, but his hand squeezes mine tightly, engulfing it completely. It feels good—safe. Like a silent promise of protection.

THE SUN'S about to set when we finally make it to what I assume is Peter's apartment building. The driver pulls up in front of a chrome-and-glass skyscraper in the exclusive Business Quarter, and Peter slides out his side of the car without a word. Before I manage to do much more than unbuckle my seatbelt, my car door opens and a large hand stretches out toward me.

I grab Peter's hand and let him pull me out onto the pavement, but when he slides his arms around me so he can lift me up, I put a hand on his chest to stop him.

"I can walk."

He frowns down at me when I, in that same moment, take a step and wince at the tenderness between my legs.

"Really," I reiterate. "I'm fine. I'll walk."

He arches an eyebrow at me, but clearly deems it not worth the fight. Without a word he puts an arm around my back for support and turns to his driver, who's also stepped out onto the pavement.

"I'll need you later tonight. Don't speak to anyone about this, not even Norman. No matter what you hear."

If the driver thinks the request odd, he doesn't show it. He just nods his head with a, "Yes, sir."

Peter puts his hand on the other man's shoulder. "Thank you, Finn," he says, his tone softer this time. "I appreciate it."

The driver—Finn—nods again. "Anytime, sir."

We walk—slowly, so my legs don't give out—through the building's front doors and across the lobby, where a porter greets Peter with a polite, "Good evening, sir."

The alpha by my side nods his greeting in return, steering me to the gilded elevators in the center of the lobby.

"Penthouse?" I ask once the doors slide closed behind us and Peter presses the button to the top floor.

He grunts in confirmation, and I smirk. "How very non-left wing of you."

Judging by the look he gives me, my joking is not appreciated. I smile brightly at him in return.

Peter's apartment is just as spectacular as the outside of the building promised.

He lets us both inside and takes me into a living room that could house my entire apartment three times. It's got large floor-to-ceiling windows offering a jaw-dropping view of the setting sun over Mattenburg and the river, and I make a bee-line for them. I've never seen the city like this—so beautiful.

"I wanted to say thank you."

I'm still looking out the window at the city and the sky aflame with orange and gold, but I can sense him shifting behind me at my words.

"*'Thank you'?*" he asks, his tone incredulous.

"Yes." I look at him over my shoulder and see his brows are still drawn in a deep frown. "You didn't have to come for me, but you did. You didn't have to sacrifice your career for me... but you did. A *'thank you'* seems in order, don't you think?"

Peter breathes out deeply, the rush of air leaving his lungs sounding like a weary sigh. He walks up behind me then, placing one large hand on my shoulder. "Of course I came for you, Leigh. It was never a choice." His breath brushes over the nape of my neck, where the bruise he left yesterday is still present. "I've had no such luxury since I first laid eyes on you."

"Don't sound so thrilled," I quip as I lean my head back against his wide chest. Every instinct in my body purrs at feeling his warm, solid form behind me, like he's my own, personal sentinel. "You seemed pretty pleased about the whole thing when you broke into my apartment for a midnight romp."

"And *you* sound remarkably calm," he says, a hint of suspicion in his voice.

I shrug, still basking in the beauty of the setting sun. "I guess I am. Calm, I mean. There's no point in fighting this, whatever it is, anymore. No one's ever been there for me like you were today. Not that I get myself kidnapped every other day or anything, but... I've never had anyone who'd stick their neck out for me."

A rumbling noise vibrates deep in his chest, and I can't tell if it's a laugh or a growl. "What happened to calling me a killer?"

I shrug. "There's something about being tied up and told you'll be fish food that can put things into perspective. I'd much rather you kill bad people than let me get hurt. Besides, you're not nearly as scary without the mask."

This time, he sighs, and it contains so much pain that I finally tear my gaze from the beautiful scenery so I can turn around and look at him.

He looks... lost, and for the first time since he came for me, I feel a sliver of unease. "Peter?"

"I'm still an alpha," he says, as if that explains everything. When I reach up to touch his face, he grasps my hand and presses it against his cheek.

"Yeah," I agree, because I don't know what else to say, and it doesn't look like he's planning on elaborating. "You are."

And then I raise up on my tiptoes and press a gentle kiss to his lips.

He responds on instinct, and I hum in appreciation when his mouth opens against mine. My arms wrap around his strong body of their own accord, and he takes me into his embrace in response, holding me so wonderfully close.

We kiss for several minutes, but for once it's slow and leisurely, with no hint of sexual urgency. I let myself get lost in the blissful knowledge from instincts far older than I, whispering to me that I am finally whole. Just like at the motel room, my very being thrums with the sensation of letting myself fuse with the man every cell in my body has ached for since our gazes met.

When he finally pulls back, the sun has set.

"I'll order dinner. Do you like sushi?"

I blink, the sudden change of topic killing some of the buzz from what was undoubtedly the best kiss of my life. "Uh... yeah. I do."

Only when he pulls out his phone and calls up to order our food does my stomach finally settle down to remind me that I haven't eaten all day. The loud, protesting growl that follows makes Peter raise an eyebrow at me mid-order. As if it's my fault the kidnappers didn't serve lunch.

AS I EAT my sushi next to the silent, broody alpha, I can't help but think back to after the first time we met. How he angrily questioned who I worked for, as if I'd

Presented in the middle of the press conference specifically to take down the Liberals.

If only I'd known then who he really was, it might have made more sense.

"Is it different for you?" I ask, pausing with a maki roll halfway to my mouth.

"Is what different?" He looks at me from his seat next to me on the couch, both eyebrows slightly raised in question.

"The instincts. I never even considered I might... you know, Present, and all that jazz. It was never something I thought I had to prepare myself for, because I never... expected to be with an alpha." I manage to stop myself from telling him I never *wanted* to be with an alpha. Funny, really. Yesterday I wouldn't have given a single, flying fuck if I hurt his feelings. Probably didn't really expect him to have any. But today... it's different.

He sighs deeply and slumps back in the sofa, arms sprawled out against the backrest. "I guess. I grew up with the knowledge that it could happen—I just never expected it to happen to *me*. I always swore it wouldn't."

I blink in surprise. "Really? You seemed... all-in, after the park. Minus the need to hide your identity from me, of course."

"I realized there wasn't anything I could do about it. Before the park, I thought I could fight it. That it was just biological manipulation and that I could reason my way out of it. I thought I was following you to find out who you were working for." He snorts, an amused sound, but his face remains blank. "Turns out I was just placating the instincts telling me I had to be near you. After the park... I was pissed. At you, for ruining every resolve I've had since I Presented as alpha once I hit puberty, and at myself for being so goddamn weak.

"I tried to stay away, but I couldn't think of anything but you. And then I found out your job was in jeopardy, and... well, I'm sure you know the jokes about alphas' need to keep their woman with pretty things. The thought of you without money for even food or rent was sickening. So I found a way to get you on the guest list for the masquerade."

"Wait." I stare at him, more shocked by that latest revelation than anything else. "You invited me to *help* me, not to take the heat off yourself after all the bad press you got when I Presented?"

Peter shrugs. "I'll admit, it was a rather nice cherry on top, but no. My main concern was for your financial stability. Of course, I'd much rather have just forced you to move in with me so I could provide directly for you, but... I might be at my instincts' mercy when it comes to you, but you seemed like an independent woman."

"That's..." I struggle to find the right words. I know enough about alphas to know they don't often look for independence in their women. That's a very large part of why I've always detested them. "Why? I've never heard of any other alpha who—"

"Who doesn't keep his female chained to his side?" He sounds bitter, his sensual lips flattening to a line. "It's funny—ever since I saw you, I finally get why so many of you are scared of us. You have no idea how badly I ache to possess you—to *own* you. It's like this clawing, snarling darkness inside, and it *hurts* every time you're not with me. I don't even really know you, and yet every thought I've had since our eyes locked has been about how I can make you mine. Make you submit to me in every way.

"I'm sure there's some poetic justice in this. I'll freely admit my campaign has been largely based on pandering to the masses' unease of the latent aggression in alphas. And now... I'm exactly what they fear. What *you* feared, from our very first meeting. A brute who acts on instincts first, with no regards for anyone else. Not even the woman I'm apparently hard-wired to care for."

I arch an eyebrow at this much honesty coming out of a politician in one go, but I can't bring myself to tease him. He's clearly far more distraught about our situation than I ever imagined. He seemed so sure of himself in the park and in my bedroom—even in the motel room—that I never stopped to wonder if maybe he was even less thrilled about our inexplicable connection than I.

"I'm... sorry?" It comes out like more of a question than I planned.

He grimaces, a half-amused expression, and reaches out for my cheek with a large hand. The heat from it as he gently strokes my skin is soothing, and I sigh with pleasure. Yeah, we're both slaves to these instincts.

"The lamb apologizes to the lion for being so irresistible? What an odd turn of events."

I flash him a grin. "Who says you're the lion?"

"Hmm," he hums, clearly not in the mood to argue what's a moot point anyway. We both know that out of the two of us, he's the predator. Even if he's apparently somewhat conflicted about it.

When he lets his hand fall from my cheek and leans back into the couch, I finish my last piece of sushi and—not waiting for an invitation—snuggle up against him.

He stiffens, probably from surprise.

"It's been a really long day," I say by way of explanation. "Can we just... pretend like everything's not a mess for tonight?"

There's a small pause before he grunts his assent. The weight of his arms settles around my body, and I smile into his shirt at the sense of calm flooding my system.

This is what it's meant to be like, I can tell. I might not know anything about alpha customs, but my body does. And right now, it knows that all is right in the world because I can hear my alpha's deep, slow breathing and feel the strength of his muscles against me.

"How come you're like this?"

"Hmm?" From the now relaxed quality in Peter's voice, I can tell our closeness is having the same effect on him as it does on me.

"Fighting against your instincts to possess me? You say you went out of your way to provide for me while letting me keep my independence. And that night, in the park... you let me go. If you knew... If me Presenting for you like that really means that... we have a connection—how come you didn't force me to stay with you? Most alphas would have. You know they would."

His chest moves underneath me with his deep, responding sigh. At first, he doesn't say anything, and I think he's going to ignore me.

"My dad was an alpha." His tone is soft now, and a little hesitant, and I get the impression he's never talked about what he's about to tell me. "And a great father to me. But not a great husband. The first time he met my mother, he knew she was the one. Could smell it. So he stalked her, like we do when we're crazy for a female, and used his alpha scent and charm to get her into bed.

"That first night, he put his claiming mark on her, making her his wife in the eyes of the law. He was... very dominating. He loved her, I know that much, but his need to possess her was so intense he never let her so much as go to the store without him. And she... From what my dad's told me, and from pictures I've seen, she was a very vibrant woman in her youth. I always knew her as a shadow of a person, like she'd been kept and dominated for so long she lost herself to his possessiveness.

"I always swore I'd never do that to a woman I claimed to love."

I touch the bruises on the back of my neck from where he bit me last night.

He sees my movement and sighs again. "Yeah. The second night with you and I nearly broke my own damn promise. Turns out I was too hard on my old man—when it comes down to it, I'm no better than him. Than any of them."

"You stopped yourself," I remind him.

"This time," he says.

I bite my lower lip as I let my fingertips slide over the raised flesh. Right now, it doesn't seem like the worst idea to be tied to the man whose mere presence can make me relax so completely, and whose touch heats my body like no other. But... I know that somewhere behind the fog of hormonal bliss is still my rational side. The side that takes such great pride in being self-sufficient and would cause me to wither like his mother did by being subjected to an alpha's unrelenting possessiveness.

"Purr for me." I bury my face against his chest and breathe in deeply. Tomorrow I can worry about how to have a relationship with a man who's blatantly stated he wants to own and possess me and keep me away from the world. Tonight I just want to pretend for a little while longer. "Please."

If he finds the request odd, he doesn't say. Soft lips press against the top of my head, and then that wonderful, deep purr rumbles out from his chest, vibrating through my bones and into my very soul. His alpha purr—the sound created to soothe and comfort me like nothing else in this world. I close my eyes and let myself relax in his embrace.

We sit like that for what feels like the better part of an hour, and I've halfway dozed off when the chirp of his phone brings me back to full consciousness with a start.

His purr cuts off as he fishes out his phone and reads the text, and a frown makes its way to his forehead.

"Bad news?" I ask, still semi-drowsy from his purring comfort.

Peter's lips flatten. "The video's out."

"Oh." I'd forgotten. I'd actually forgotten the grotesque video we'd been forced to shoot that morning—and what the point of it was: to ruin Leod for good. "Was that someone from your staff freaking out?"

"Yup." He rubs his face and sits up, gently easing out from underneath me until he's perched at the edge of the sofa. "I have to go deal with this."

"Oh." I bite my lip and straighten up myself. "Is there any chance you won't have to withdraw from the election?"

"No. There won't be a person left in Mattenburg who'd ever vote for me. The Liberals have to distance themselves from me to have a shot at recovering before the next election."

Feeling somewhat awkward now that reality has forced its way into our small bubble of peace, I glance up at him. "Do you... want me to come with you?"

He looks at me then, and the frown on his forehead softens. Gently, he cups my cheek with a hand and strokes my skin with his thumb. "No, my sweet. You've been through enough. In fact..." He hesitates, and I can see the strain passing over his face before he steels his features and looks at me with that emotionless expression he usually employs when I've seen him on TV in the past.

Then he withdraws his hand from my face and clasps it in his lap. "This will be the last time we see each other."

It takes me a moment to grasp what he says. When I do, it feels like the bottom's dropped out of my stomach.

"W-what?"

There's regret in his gray eyes, but also determination as he looks at me. "You have to leave the city. It's not safe for you here—not when Bremen knows you're my weakness. And you're not safe from me, either. If you stay, it's only a matter of time before I put a claiming mark on you."

He gets up and turns his back on me, fiddling with his phone as he does. "I'll arrange for one of my trusted people to pick you up tonight, before I get back."

"Peter—" I get up too, my brows knitting in confusion —and hurt.

"It's for the best, Leigh. The only thing I want more than to possess you is to make sure you're safe. So I have to send you away. I'm not a good man—you know this. I'll take you, and I'll *break* you. Get out now, before it's too late."

"*Peter!*" I say again, because I can't believe he's actually doing this. I may not know much about alpha customs, but I do know that this is all wrong—every newly-awakened instinct in my body has known it since I first locked eyes with him: we are meant to be together. He can't just walk away from this—from *us*.

Except he does.

"I'll send you money every month. You won't lack for

anything. Be safe, Leigh." Peter Leod gives me one final, lingering look before he crosses the floor and disappears into the hallway. Seconds later, I hear the door close shut behind him.

He's gone.

FIFTEEN

I should be happy.

I never wanted anything to do with an alpha in the first place, and especially not a scheming politician who moonlights as a stalker-cum-murderer. I've seen enough of how alphas treat their women to know the smart thing to do is to stay away. Heck, after having been subjected to it myself... He's manipulated me from the start, and I don't just mean my hormones. Sending me a ticket to the masquerade without letting me know the invitation came from him? Pretending like he had no idea why I was there when he caught me snooping--and later forcing his way into my home to *"claim his payment"*? All actions of a complete psychopath.

But... there is no denying how he's thrown away his entire career to save me. Nor how good it feels when I'm in his arms—how right.

I know he felt the same way too, in the deepest part of

my being. And still, he's chosen to give up on me. And *send me away.*

Who does he even think he is? A refreshing burst of anger floods through my veins and washes away the numbness of my shock over his abrupt departure out of my life.

An alpha, is the obvious answer. He's so used to being obeyed without question that even in his attempt at protecting me from harm he's completely disregarding anything I might have to say on the subject. *High-handed alpha jerk.*

I love Mattenburg, despite its many faults, and I love my job. Does he really just think he can toss all I've worked so hard to achieve away because *he* deems it the best option?

The obvious answer is yes—yes, he does, and it infuriates me. He didn't even talk to me about his decision—just let me snuggle up against him as if everything was going to be okay, like it was going to be us against the world like every instinct in my body is telling me it's *meant* to be... Only to pull the proverbial rug from underneath me the next moment and tell me we'll never see each other again.

Well, if Mr. High-and-Mighty Alpha thinks the woman he called *mate* less than eight hours ago is just going to meekly pack her stuff and leave because *he's* decreed it, he's got another think coming.

I've not had any time to see how Mattenburg's reacted to the undercover article I did on the masquerade, what with being kidnapped and made to shoot a perverted porn video with the Liberals' leading candidate, but I'm pretty damn sure the city's in uproar. No one knew the kind of depraved shit the city's elite got up to behind closed doors, and judging by the unrest in the streets as Leod's driver drove us to his building, the citizens are on the brink of revolting.

My biology may have selected Leod as my... my *mate*, but I'm first and foremost a reporter. I'm not about to turn tail and run because his enemies see me as an easy target. Mattenburg's been thrown into the biggest power vacuum in recent history, and if anyone can stop Bremen from snatching up the reins again in the turmoil following the people's champion being slandered as a rapist, it's me.

Not Leod. Not Roy, my editor. Not some other, big alpha. *Me.*

I take a deep breath and grab the TV remote from the coffee table in front of me. It's time to see exactly what I have to deal with.

"...shocking video that appears to be a genuine recording of the Liberals' mayoral candidate, Peter Leod, brutally raping a tied-up young woman. The video comes as a huge blow to the Liberal party, who just this morning were looking at an unprecedented uptick in the polls after the anonymous leak of savage alpha rituals taking place behind the annual masquerade's closed doors.

"Leod has yet to make a statement, but Lord Mayor Bremen has called for an emergency press conference to discuss what he calls the current issues. There hasn't been an agenda released, but all political commentators expect

Leod to, at a minimum, be forced to step down. Some have even predicted that the public call for jail time is a very real possibility for the previously beloved politician.

"The last twelve hours have seen an uproar from a population already uneasy about the undeniably alpha core in the city's power structure. Who'll step in to calm the waters is yet undecided, but all experts point to this video being a godsend for the Lord Mayor. With no real opposition to take Leod's place, the city's got no one else to turn to to prevent a full-scale revolt.

"And now, if you've just tuned in, here's a clip from the video. Be warned that it does contain what some might call objectionable material. Viewer discretion is advised."

I watch, fist clenched around the remote, as Leod's large flat screen TV flashes the words, *"Warning: Extreme sexual content,"* in red across a black screen before it tunes into a close-up of Leod's face.

His teeth are gritted and his pupils blown, the poster image of a rampaging alpha. It takes a couple of seconds before the sound catches up to the visuals, and his hoarse grunts and the wet slapping of flesh fills the room, mixed with muffled whimpering. The video slowly zooms out, and it takes everything I've got not to turn off the TV.

The woman on the bed underneath Leod is very clearly me—anyone who's even vaguely familiar with me would be able to recognize my face from the shot.

Seeing myself fucked like a whore and broadcast for all to see is unexpectedly humiliating, and I have to fight back tears as I stare at the screen. Yeah, I can understand why everyone who's watched this video would assume I was unwilling. Not only am I tied up and sobbing into the pillow underneath me, but the visual of a huge alpha on top of my much smaller body, forcing me to take his enormous cock so hard and fast the bed shakes for every thrust, is shocking.

When the video zooms into where his brutal length is pistoning in and out of my weakly struggling body, it's clear my pussy's struggling with his girth. It's red and swollen, and clings desperately to his cock on every outstroke.

Out of the shot, my sobs become more frantic, and it's soon obvious why. The man holding the camera moves behind us, showing a full close-up of my widely gaped entrance swallowing Leod's cock, where the swelling at the bottom of his member is visible. He's about to knot, and my poor pussy already looks like it's been stretched far beyond what it's meant to take.

In the present, my body shivers as I remember exactly what it felt like when my alpha knotted me only hours ago. It might look—and sound—like I'm in agony, but the pleasure from taking it was like what I imagine a hit of top-quality Ecstasy is like. The physical pleasure of being forced to gape open wide enough to take an alpha knot might be mixed with pain, but the endorphin high is indescribable.

Plus... lying with him after, while he purrs and tends to me like I'm the most precious entity in the entire universe, is the closest I've ever been to feeling truly loved.

I'm stopped from further contemplation of the weird warmth in my chest at that thought when my own wail rips through the apartment. One glance at the screen and I can't stop myself from wincing. Leod's knot is fully inside my now wildly spasming pussy, and even from the close-up of our genitals, it's obvious that I'm struggling underneath him. I don't remember doing that, but then again... taking a knot has a tendency to make it pretty damn hard to retain detailed memories.

I force myself to turn off the TV again, not the least in the mood to hear the news anchor comment further on my now humiliatingly public knotting. There's an urge rising in me, one that says I ought to follow Leod's command and hide out in his apartment until someone can come and get me. Someone who can take me away from the city, where I'm now the face for women victimized by alphas all over the world. The more I think about how Mattenburg's population is watching me get screwed to pieces on screen, the more that urge grows.

But... if I do that, I won't only be leaving Peter to the wolves—I'll also allow Mattenburg to fall back into the hands of the man who would have had me killed without a second thought, had Peter not showed up.

And there's no way in hell I'll ever let that happen.

SIXTEEN

I manage to hail a taxi from the street underneath Leod's apartment and huddle up in the backseat trying not to make eye contact. Luckily the driver is too busy listening to the news to pay any attention to me.

"Where to, Miss?" he says without turning down the volume on the radio station blaring on about, *"Peter Leod raping a poor girl, and where is she anyway? Did he kill her to keep her quiet?"*

"155 Tower Avenue. Then Town Hall."

"Going down for the protest, huh? Would myself, but gotta feed the kids. Fucking alphas, keeping every beta down and raping our women."

I make a noncommittal noise he takes for agreement, and soon we're on our way. It takes half an hour to make it to my apartment. I tell the driver I'll be down in five minutes, and rush upstairs to grab my wallet, phone, press badge, and a hat.

He's still waiting for me with the radio blaring, this time about the protest taking place in front of Town Hall in the lead-up to the emergency press conference. Thankfully he's too preoccupied with the news to notice my quick wardrobe change. The hat was a last-minute addition, and my best chance at getting into Town Hall without anybody recognizing me.

The roads leading to Town Hall are less blocked by traffic than when Leod's driver took us through downtown, but when we get within three blocks, my taxi comes to a stop. When I look out the window I see an ever-growing crowd of milling people in front of us, completely blocking the road. The radio's blaring is the only reason I didn't notice the angry shouts coming from outside the taxi sooner.

"Sorry, miss, can't get you all the way. You'll have to join the march a little sooner."

"Yeah, sure. Thanks." I fish out payment for the fare and hand it to him. Just as I do, our eyes meet in the rear view mirror.

"Hey! Aren't you—"

I open the backseat door and throw myself out into the throng of people before he can complete his question. The crowd of protesters quickly swallows me up.

It takes me longer than what I'd have liked to fight my way through the crowd the three blocks to Town Hall, and I keep frantically glancing at my watch. Three to ten, and I'm still a block away. According to the radio, the press conference is due to start at ten sharp.

I make it to the square in front of Town Hall five minutes past, and the crowd here is so thick it's hard to force my way through the irate people shouting a mixture of anti-alpha abuse at the police—most of whom are alphas themselves—lined up in front of the main entrance, riot shields at the ready. Up on the side of the building, there's a big screen displaying the Lord Mayor on the podium, addressing the gathered reporters, but the shouts out here are too loud for me to hear what he's saying. In the background, I can see Leod standing alongside other politicians from his party. His eyes are downcast and his shoulders tense.

It's sheer force of will that lets me elbow my way through the people up front until I'm finally able to slip underneath a shouting woman's arm, leaving me face-to-face with a grimly determined-looking police officer on the other side of his riot shield.

I don't bother shouting an explanation, just slap my press badge against the clear shield and point at the door behind him.

"You're late!" he barks, but when someone shoves against my back from behind so I slam up against his shield he twists his body, leaving a small gap between him and the officer next to him. I don't waste time and quickly slip through with a gasped, "Thank you."

He doesn't bother responding, his focus wholly on the crowd behind me.

I run as fast as I can up the stairs to the main entrance, waving my press badge at the security stationed there. I experience a brief flicker of relief that neither of the armed men at the door are one of the two Town Hall employees who kidnapped me—I hadn't even thought about that possibility before I saw them.

"Meeting room two," the guard who checks my badge says. "If you hurry, you should be able to make it before they drag Leod off."

I grimace and reach to take my badge back. "Thanks."

His eyes flicker down over my picture once more, and then he frowns. "Huh, you look an awful lot like the girl he banged in that video."

"I get that a lot," I say, grabbing my badge and shouldering my way past him. "Thanks."

"Hey, wait a minute!"

I don't turn around, opting instead for a flat run toward meeting room two. I've been here often enough to know the way by heart, and despite my single-minded focus on getting to that podium before one of Bremen's lackeys gets a hold of me, I can't help but notice how different the building looks from the last time I was here. No gilded tapestries cover the walls, nor are waiters handing out champagne flutes to diamond-covered guests. No, the halls are completely empty, probably because everyone from politicians to the cleaning staff are currently pressed together in meeting room two.

When I finally reach the heavy double doors, I don't pause to attempt a stealthy entrance. I only slow down long enough to rip them both open.

"...this current lack of trust with certain political figures."

I recognize Lord Mayor Bremen's voice even before I see him on the podium at the far end of the room. Every seat is filled with reporters, and behind the mayor is a row of political candidates, all with grim expressions. Peter's there too, his features surprisingly calm, considering how close he is to the man who cost him his career and reputation.

At the sound of both doors banging open, his gaze—as well as that of everyone else behind the podium—lands on me, and his eyes widen ever so slightly. No one else lingers for more than half a second, dismissing me as just a tardy reporter, but Peter doesn't take his eyes off me. Judging from his dark stare and the way he jerks his head toward the door, he wants me to turn around and leave before Bremen or any of his goons realize who I am.

Despite the spasm in my lizard brain to do as my alpha demands, I walk down the middle row leading to the podium, determined to complete what I came here for. He may be my alpha, but despite how easily my body and mind yield to him when we are together, I am still a strong, independent woman—and I have a job to do.

Only when I am a few feet from the raised podium and the row of politicians do the two goons stationed to the side of the room spot my approach. A whirl of movement in the corner of my eye makes me flinch back and whip my head around, just in time to see Peter jump down from the podium and clasp an unyielding hand around the wrist of the goon attempting to get a hold of me.

"Touch her and you lose a hand," he growls, low enough that no one else is able to hear.

The goon bares his teeth at Peter, but I don't wait for him to retaliate. Quickly skirting Peter's massive bulk while he's preoccupied with the now struggling bodyguard, I climb up on the podium.

Bremen, whose speech has faltered during the turmoil right in front of him, stares at me with thinly-veiled shock, and I flash him a smile before I grab for the microphone mounted in front of him.

"My name is Leigh Adams, and I—" my voice rings through the conference room for less than a second before the microphone is snatched back out of my hand. I spin around and see the mayor sneer down at me with thinly-veiled disgust. It seems he's finally recognized me.

But before he can say or do anything, loud voices from beyond the stage break through the silence.

"Is that—?"

"Is she—?"

"She's that girl!"

"She's the girl from the video!"

"Let her speak!"

Both Bremen and I turn to look at the crowd of reporters shouting at him to give me the microphone back. I glance up at the Lord Mayor, whose face is a study in conflicting emotions. He's obviously trying to keep a calm façade, but the rage boiling just below the surface is threatening to break through.

"This is outrageous," he says into the microphone, and I'm impressed with his ability to rein in his obvious fury enough to sound genuinely shocked and appalled. "This is a very serious press conference, not a free-for-all. Please find your seat immediately, *miss,* or you will be escorted from the building."

A chorus of protests erupts from the room in front of him.

"Mayor, let her speak!"

The phrase is repeated over and over again, and more and more reporters are getting out of their seats to vent their agitation at Bremen's reluctance to let me be heard.

His gaze sweeps over the rowdy mass of reporters, and I see in his eyes the moment he realizes he can't win this round. The brief look of defeat is quickly wiped away as he raises a hand to silence the room.

"Fine. As you wish. The girl will speak." He gives me a short, but infinitely threatening glare that no one but myself and the politicians behind us would be able to see. "And I am sure she will do so knowing the consequences of speaking falsely. After all, a man's life and reputation are at stake here."

I nod shortly at him. I know what his warning means —tell stories of how he had me kidnapped, and Peter will pay the price. With his life.

The tight grip of fear that momentarily closes around my heart is an odd and unexpected sensation. Since the very first time we met, I've known on a primal level that Peter Leod was the strongest, most powerful man I'd ever know. Even in the park, surrounded by blood and broken bodies, I felt safe. Because *he* was there. The second he stepped through the motel door this morning, I knew I would make it out of there safe and sound.

Icy tendrils creep up my back at the sudden realization that, even with all Peter's strength and power, this man in front of me could - and would - harm him. Is this how Peter feels, knowing how easily his enemies could harm me to get at him? I am infinitely simpler to hurt than my alpha protector, and suddenly his attempt at sending me away makes more sense than it did just an hour ago.

As I stare up at the Lord Mayor, I know without a shadow of a doubt that if Peter dies, I will be nothing but a shell. He is my alpha—the other half of me—and it doesn't matter that I never chose him, because it never was a choice.

But if I back down now, I lose him anyway. He will send me away to keep me safe, and I will never see him again.

And that's not an option, either.

My hands are clammy when I accept the microphone from Bremen once more.

I turn around and look out over the many reporters staring back up at me. The room is so silent you could hear a pin drop.

This is my one chance. Fighting against the sick

feeling of nerves fluttering in my stomach, I lift the microphone to my lips.

"I am Leigh Adams, the girl from the video you've seen all over the news this evening. And I have something important to share with you."

SEVENTEEN

"Before I explain what happened on that tape, I need to tell you about the night I met Peter Leod." I take a deep breath as I look out over the many faces and video cameras pointed at me. There is no holding back now.

"I am the KTP reporter who Presented during the press conference a few weeks ago."

Surprised murmurs fill the room, but I ignore them.

"At the time, I didn't know why. It was the most shameful thing that's ever happened to me—until I was blasted across the city on that video tonight, of course. I was told not to show up at work again until after the election—if I was lucky. I was devastated. I've worked hard for my career and my reputation, and all of it was gone—just like that. Because my body betrayed me, without my conscious knowledge or approval.

"That next night, Peter Leod came to see me."

Another round of murmurs. I take the small break to

look down at him. He's still standing in front of the podium, alone now and facing the audience, like my own personal bodyguard. His muscles are tense as if he's expecting a fight, and I know he's scanning the room for any potential threat to me. Even though I know he doesn't want me to do this, his first instincts are still to protect me. As mine are to protect him, which is why I have to moderate the true events of the night he came for me.

"I don't need to tell anyone here how badly affected Peter's reputation was after that press conference. He's supposed to be the one alpha who protects us all—the champion of the women and beta males. Our voice. And yet there he was, broadcast across the city as nothing more than a primitive, feral beast so wrapped up in his embarrassing instincts he lost all ability to act like a civilized human being.

"It's probably no surprise, either, that when he came to see me, he was very angry at me. I thought he might hurt me for ruining his reputation.

"He didn't. That night, I learned what it means to be an alpha's mate."

This time, the voices in the room rise to more than a murmur, and I take another break as the gathered reporters come to grips with what I've implied.

"Miss Adams, are you saying you're Mr. Leod's *mate?*" someone calls out, his tone incredulous.

"No, I am not saying that. Not yet." Subconsciously, I reach up to touch the bite marks hidden by my hair. "He has yet to claim me. You see, for him to court me like an alpha would his intended mate, there would be no possible way of repairing his image as the moderate Liberal who does not support archaic gender roles and biological structures. And I... I was scared of him. Of the alpha in him. The man you saw fighting amidst every other alpha in the room during that press conference is the Peter Leod I've come to know. He tries to hide his physique in those expensive, tailored suits and behind smooth words to make you forget what he is underneath the thin layer of civilization. Because he knows, as well as every other politician in here, that we fear them—the alphas.

"And we are more than happy to play along, aren't we? Every one of us in here can smell the alpha pheromones in the air, but we all pretend like we don't notice. We pretend like it doesn't fuck with our own hormones and instincts, we pretend that we're all too civilized to let our behavior be dictated by our biology. Even the Conservatives, with their old-ways agenda, hide the most primal of their urges to not show us their true faces, and with good reason. We all saw what kind of pleasure these politicians—these *alphas*—seek during this year's masquerade. And we were horrified. Appalled.

"These men up here with me are the people we entrust with upholding the very foundations of our society, and every single one of them partook in the auction at the masquerade. Every single one gave in to his most primal urges—everything we as a society claim we want no part of.

"That's what Peter did to me in the video you've now all seen. He gave in to his instincts, and he took me as an alpha takes his woman. But it wasn't rape—I wanted every moment of it."

I fasten my gaze on Leod's as the murmur rises anew across the room. It's only a short moment before he turns his head back to scour the crowd, but it's long enough for me to see the pride in his eyes. It gives me strength to continue.

"We allow ourselves to be blinded by the masks these men wear to gain our confidence, but deep down we all know what they are. And we crave it on a primal level so ingrained in our DNA we hardly realize it's there. But it is. There's a reason why every politician in this city is an alpha, why every riot officer and firefighter is one of them. We gravitate toward them because everything inside of us yearns to follow a strong alpha. We may play at being civilized, but deep down, we still have the same urges and instincts as we did tens of thousands of years ago.

"Peter Leod didn't rape me. What you've seen is a private video tape of consensual sex with an alpha. I don't know who leaked this video, or how they got a hold of it, but I do know it's been done in an attempt at discrediting the only man in this city who speaks up against the corruption and unfair segregations in our community.

"Do not hold Peter Leod's nature against him when you don't hold it against every alpha who's ever knotted a woman, and every beta or female who happily follows them. Do not punish him for what he is—hold him accountable for what he says and what he does, like you should any candidate hoping to lead our city. That is the only way to put a stop to the deceitful doings by corrupt men with too much power and too little respect for the people they are meant to serve. Do not blame their alpha nature for your distrust. If you do, you will only give them excuses. Blame their actions. Blame their ill intent. Hold them accountable not for what they are, but for what they do. And then *act* on it.

"Do not turn against the only hope Mattenburg has for ending the corruption."

My heart is hammering in my chest when I finally finish my speech. I never wanted this kind of attention, but now that I have it, I desperately hope that I've done enough to save Peter. And Mattenburg.

Movement in my peripheral vision makes me turn my head in time to see Lord Mayor Bremen—with a face like a thunder cloud—stalk toward me, and it takes all I've got not to shrink back from his obvious anger. Clearly, he's not impressed with my speech, even though I didn't mention his involvement in that video directly.

But before the pissed alpha reaches me—and the microphone—Peter appears by my side, undoubtedly summoned by the aggressive pheromones in the air. He wraps an arm around my shoulders and shoots Bremen a pointed look, a clear warning, before he turns us both toward the crowd once more.

"Mr. Leod, is what she's saying true?" a reporter shouts above the loud mutterings from the room.

Peter glances down at me, and his gaze softens as our eyes lock. Gently, he touches a hand to my chin before returning his attention to the reporter. "Every word. And she's right—it's about time we stop pretending. I am an alpha, with every instinct and desire that goes along with it. And it changes nothing. I will still fight for equal rights and elimination of corruption in Mattenburg, like I have from day one. I will fight for the people of this city, not its crooked elite. I am every firefighter, every policeman and every bodyguard in this city. I am here to protect you, and I will not rest until the people of Mattenburg are safe. I am an alpha, yes, and my power is yours. This I swear to you."

IT'S midnight before Peter finally manages to leave the heaving throng of reporters and politicians with excuses that "his mate" is falling asleep on her feet. He's not far off—when the door to his office finally shuts behind us, I stagger the few feet to the nearest armchair and collapse in it.

"I'm so tired I think I could sleep for a week," I mumble, my eyes already sliding shut.

"You've had a long day," Peter says, his voice a deep rumble. Its sound relaxes muscles I wasn't aware were tight. He walks over to my chair, easily lifts me up so he can sit, and then places me in his lap. He's warm and safe, and I nuzzle in against his strong body with a pleased mewl.

"Before you sleep, may I ask you how you came up with that speech? You creamed my PR team with that show, and I pay them an awful lot of money to make me look good."

I shrugged, not bothering to open my eyes. "I just told the truth. Your willingness to give me up to protect me, even from yourself, kinda proved that you're one of the few good guys in this city, deep down. You're the reason that what goes on at the masquerade is public knowledge, after all."

A small pause. "You do know I did that solely for selfish reasons, right?"

I smile against his chest at the somewhat hesitant note to his voice, as if he's reluctant to admit it to me. "Eh, either way, you acted in the best interest of the public. And I think as long as someone's there to remind you to keep doing that, you'll make a most excellent Lord Mayor. So I guess I better stick around to keep you on the right path."

"Leigh... it's not safe. If Bremen gets a hold of you again, he isn't gonna use you as blackmail. You're smart, and the way you spoke to the city tonight, he knows you'll be a threat to him in your own right. I won't have you harmed. You understand?" This time, there's more than a hint of grim determination in his tone, and I know he's working himself up to be all Protective Alpha and attempt to send me away again.

I give his chest a soothing pat. "I guess you better make sure I'm protected, then, 'cause I'm not leaving Mattenburg. Or you. You may be my alpha, but you don't get to boss me around outside of the bedroom. The sooner you accept that, the happier you'll be."

He's silent for several seconds, until a defeated sigh escapes him. A large hand cradles the back of my head, pulling me in closer against his bulk. "You better prepare yourself to never leave the bedroom, Miss Adams."

I smile against his shirt and cuddle into his warm embrace. "I'm sure we can come to a mutually satisfying agreement, *Mr. Leod.*"

EIGHTEEN

2 WEEKS LATER

The bang of the front door slamming shut rouses me from my sleep.

I blink a couple of times into the dimmed light in Peter's living room—or *our* living room, as it is now—and sit up on the soft leather couch I've fallen asleep on while waiting for Peter to come home.

A large, dark figure stands in the door opening between the living room and the hallway. A man—and alpha—judging by his sheer size and bulk. He stands there silently, looking at me from the shadows concealing his face.

"Peter?" I ask, still groggy from sleep.

He moves toward me, and when the faint light from the city outside flickers through the blinds onto his face, I realize it's not just the shadows hiding his face—it's also a now familiar, black mask.

"You jerk!" I hiss, pressing my hand against my chest

as my heart settles back down again from the involuntary lurch at the unexpected presence of a potential stranger. "I thought we were done with masks and lurking in the shadows."

He doesn't answer, but before I can lay into him for being a prick, he reaches the couch and bends to press his lips against mine.

If I hadn't already recognized his mask, I would have known him by this kiss. It's soft but so unquestionably needy, filled with heat and a longing that resonates deep in my own bones. No one's ever kissed me like Peter, and no one ever will.

My alpha.

Even though he's still an ass for creeping up on me like that.

"If you want to roleplay rapey stalker, give a girl a head's up beforehand," I grumble against his lips. "I don't particularly want to go back to the good old days of thinking I'm gonna get murdered by some creepy idiot in a mask."

From the twist of his lips against mine and the rumble deep in his chest, I can tell he's amused, but instead of replying—or pulling back—he crawls up on the couch, pushing me down flat on my back without breaking our kiss.

Strong hands pull my pajamas pants and panties down over my hips, ripping the elastic as he tugs them off me completely. I moan softly into his mouth, my arousal waking with a start as he delves a couple of fingers down between my thighs, stroking me open.

I shudder and gasp when he finds my clit, my own hands grasping for his strong shoulders. I dimly recognize the sturdy high-tech fabric he wore in the park underneath my fingertips, but my attention swiftly returns to my sex.

Peter rubs my sensitive little nub between two fingertips, stroking up and down with small movements until I'm squirming and panting underneath him. My pussy is aching to be opened, and I cant my hips up in invitation. He takes it, easily sliding first one, and then another finger inside my already wet opening.

"Jesus, that's…" The rest of my sentence dies on a groan, because just then he forces a third digit into my already stretched sheath. He's only bedded me twice since we were forced to record that awful video, the long hours during and immediately after the election not leaving us many moments alone, and my body's still not entirely adjusted to his ruthless size. A problem he's apparently planning on rectifying tonight.

Not that I'm complaining.

Peter pumps his three fingers into me in a steady rhythm, driving soft squelches from my weeping channel every time his knuckles breach my entrance. When his thumb finds its place on my clit, rubbing circles across the little pearl, I dig my nails into his shoulders and pant harder. He's not easing me into it, and soon I'm squirming for his skilled hand as he forces my body to climb.

When he changes the angle to get my G-spot, I surrender.

"Oh, God, fuck! Peter!" I cry out, a long, drawn-out moan as my pussy clenches hard around the invasion and every nerve ending in my lower body crackles with white-hot pleasure. My orgasm is deep and long, and oh-so-satisfying, and when Peter pulls his fingers from me I collapse into a satisfied puddle on the couch.

"That was—*oh!*" My sleepy appreciation is abruptly interrupted when the masked alpha grabs me by the waist so he can lift me over the back of the couch. He spins me around, and then a large hand between my shoulderblades presses me forward until I am bent over the back of the couch, ass up and face halfway down into the soft cushions.

The hand he doesn't have on my back he uses to cup my pussy from behind, making me spread my thighs wider to accommodate him. His palm is hot against my pulsing sex, and I arch my back in an instinctive plea for him to slip his fingers back inside of me.

"Don't move." It is a rough growl, filled with heat and darkness, and it makes a shiver of anticipation run up my spine.

Slowly, provokingly, he rubs his thick digits between my splayed lips, teasing my entrance and tickling my still-hardened clit with the tip of his fingers.

I mewl and try to press my mound against him harder, but before I can get any sort of stimulation, he abruptly moves both hands from me and steps back.

"What—" I turn my head, about to raise up, but his sharp command whips through the room, making my nipples harden and more liquid drizzle out from my eagerly upturned pussy.

"Don't. Move."

I freeze in place, but keep my eyes on his dark-clad figure just barely visible in my periphery.

"Don't you wanna knot me, Lord Mayor?" I surprise myself with the sultry tone to my voice, more so than I do the question itself. A few weeks ago, I dreaded the harsh stretch of his brutal knot, but now... as I stand bent over the sofa in the darkened space of his living room, bare from the waist down, open and ready for my alpha to mount... the thought of it makes the deepest, most primal parts of me shiver with longing.

When he ties with me, we are fully one. When he shoves that thick, hard knot through my protesting opening and lodges it up against my aching G-spot, there is nothing else in this world. Just him, and me, and that deep, full sensation of completion beyond my wildest dreams.

With him, I lose myself, only to be reborn again while he holds me in his arms and purrs his deep devotion in my ear.

And right now, that's all I need.

But Peter doesn't answer me. He walks out of the room, leaving me aching for his touch.

I breathe deeply and grasp at the backrest. As much as I want him *right now,* I'm also intrigued to see what he's got planned. I squeeze my thighs together to ease the hollow need between them, hoping he'll be back soon.

He is.

He's nearly soundless as he steps back into the living room and crosses the floor, and as so many times before I am awed at his lithe movements for such a huge man. He moves like a large panther, and I am once again reminded of the predator so deeply ingrained in his DNA.

I catch a glimpse of what looks like a jar of Vaseline before he disappears behind me again, and a flutter of worry makes my stomach knot. Surely, he wouldn't...?

A flicker of light straight ahead distracts me from my uneasy thoughts, and I frown as the TV comes to life. Peter changes the channel to the 24-hour news station and throws the remote on the couch in front of me. From the sounds of it, it seems they're discussing inner-city school programs.

"What...?" I squint, confused, at the screen. "You want to watch the *news,* while we...?"

My only answer is the slick sound of some form of lubrication being rubbed on flesh, and my previous concerns return with an uncomfortable twinge in my gut.

"Er, you're not going to... I don't want to do... only vaginal, right? You're way too big for—"

The massive man behind me leans forward, and I can feel the warmth from his body against my back even though he's not touching me.

"Trust me." Those two words brush against my ear in a soft caress. It's not quite a whisper, but it's not a command, either. He touches his lips to my hair, lets his hand trail down my back, over my upturned backside and down my hamstring. "I will never hurt you, Leigh."

I breathe in deeply, taking in his calming alpha pheromones, and feel the beginning knot of anxiety melt away like snow on a warm spring day. In the deepest parts of me I know he's telling me the truth.

His hand ventures back up from my hamstring and slips in between my thighs to rub gently at my clit. I doesn't take long for the hot waves of pleasure to set in, and I moan softly as I rock back against his touch.

It's all the invitation he needs to take things further. Fingers slick with Vaseline slip into my waiting sheath, pumping slowly.

I moan again and close my eyes against the pleasure of feeling him inside of me, even if it isn't the part of him I crave most. He pushes another finger into me, and that delicious stretch that has my toes curling against the parquet floor sets in. Three, I guess, from the times he's fingered me before. But they move more easily in me than normal, thanks to the lubrication he's smeared on them.

"Remember when Bremen's men forced me to tie you up?"

My eyes pop open at the reminder, and I frown at the TV screen. Why on Earth does he want to talk about that now? "Y-yeah?" My breath catches as his fingertips strum over my G-spot.

"You told me you wanted me to, because you trusted me." His voice rumbles through the darkened room, making my nipples ache with the unmistakable signs of his own arousal.

"Y-*yes?*" This time, my voice pitches higher at the end, because just as I say it, another finger forces its way into my already stretched pussy. "Fuck, *Peter...!*" Four. That's more than he's ever given me before, and despite the Vaseline, I buck against the pressure in vain protest until he pinches my clit with his free hand. A sharp shock of bliss makes me tighten around his intruding digits, sending warm tendrils of heat through my abdomen. His cock— and knot—are thicker than this, and despite the difference in sensation at being penetrated by his fingers, my pussy gives in to him with a wet spasm. "Ooh, God, that's so good...."

"And yet, when they suggested I fist you, you refused," he continues, his voice calm despite the dark notes of unadulterated lust rolling off his tongue. The slick sound of his lubricated fingers working my pussy are a constant, dirty undertone as I clench my hands around the backrest of the couch and try to focus on what he's saying.

"You refused *me*. Am I to take it your trust in me has limits?"

A worrying notion of what, exactly, he's planning finally cuts through to my conscious mind, and I try to straighten up from my bent-over position. "Don't be silly —you've just got ridiculously big hands, and—*ooh G-ngh!*"

My protest is interrupted by a long, drawn-out moan when he digs his fingertips straight into my G-spot. My thighs tremble, and I slump forward again to clamp onto the backrest so I don't lose my footing, panting from the onslaught of sensation melting every muscle down below.

"My hands are no bigger than my knot." It's all he says before I feel more pressure at my entrance, and then his thumb forces my already stretched lips to their limits.

Five. He's got five fingers in me, and it feels like he's going to break me in half.

"No, Peter—ngh-*ooh!*" My panicked protest dies on a groan as he rubs my clit with the hand not trying to force its way inside of me. I toss my head back against the ruthless pleasure bursting through my pelvis, simultaneously trying to press my mound against his touch and away from his brutal penetration.

He doesn't let me escape.

"Hold still." It's an alpha's command, and despite his calm tone, it still cracks against my instincts like a punishing whip. I jerk and freeze before I even realize what I'm doing.

"Good girl," he says, a hint of smugness in his voice this time.

"You prick," I pant, but without much conviction. I'm too focused on the five fingers stretching me open to have much energy left over to fight him. *"God*, why?"

"Because I need you to understand that I will never hurt you."

"I know that," I whimper, my fingers clutching desperately at the backrest. He's gently pressing further into me, and when his knuckles catch against the brutally stretched rim of my weeping pussy, I see stars. Only his now unrelenting stimulation of my hard little clit is keeping me from kicking out.

"You don't, or you wouldn't have denied me then, and you wouldn't be so scared even now."

"I'm not scared," I protest. "I just—*ah*—I just have spatial awareness!"

"You're trembling like a leaf," he states matter-of-factly, and I realize he's right. "You want me to stop, even though taking my fist will give you pleasure so intense only my knot will ever compare. You're scared, because you don't trust that I won't hurt you. And I need you to understand that you will always, *always,* be safe in my hands. I need you to know, in the very depths of your soul, that I will cherish and protect you always. That nothing and no one will ever get to harm you and live."

"And you think *fisting* me is going to do that?" It's meant as a snarky comeback, but comes out like a trembling sob.

"I know it will," he says. And then he pushes his hard knuckles through my pussy's resistance.

I scream until my voice gives out. I pound my hands against the backrest, and I buck like a wild animal in my desperate attempt at dislodging the enormous hand now stuck inside my quivering sheath, but nothing I do changes the fact that his entire hand is up inside of my pussy so deep I can feel the bones in his wrist flex against my fitfully spasming entrance.

Peter holds his hand still inside of me while I thrash

and sob in between desperate gulps of air. His other arm is wrapped around my hip, anchoring me to reality while his fingers draw gentle circles against my clit. It takes several minutes before the screaming from every single nerve in my pelvis and abdomen settles down enough that I can even sense the gentle pleasure pulsing through my nub of nerves from his almost soothing stimulation.

It's only then, when the rushing in my ears dies down and my vision clears from pure white, that I realize my body's violent response to the brutal penetration is not from agony.

Sure, there's some pain from the impossible stretch of my mercilessly gaped pussy, but not more than when he knots me. And it's a good kind of pain—the kind so laced with endorphins it's nearly impossible to separate from the deep, violent roar of pleasure thrumming through my soft tissue and pelvic bones for every frantic beat of my heart.

He's right, I think, detached amusement making me gasp out something resembling a laugh. If he doesn't hurt me by shoving his entire goddamn hand up my reluctant pussy, then nothing he could ever do to me will.

"Take a deep breath, Leigh," he rumbles behind me, and I draw in a shuddering gasp.

The hand in my sheath slowly, carefully begins to ball up, and I dig my nails into the leather of the couch and keep breathing as he forms a fist inside of me.

My pussy desperately tries to clamp down against the new pressure, but it's no match for the ruthless alpha's strength. A few seconds later he's got his hand clenched into a fully-formed fist. *Inside* of me.

A gush of liquid bursts out of my channel, soaking his arm and my inner thighs and drawing a deep growl laced with unmistakable *lust* from him.

And I... I break down in tears.

There's something so indescribably intimate about this—it's like he's holding the very essence of my being in his clenched fist, like he's reaching for my heart itself. And as I stand there, bent over his sofa in the darkened living room only lit by the TV, I finally surrender myself to him completely.

I've been scared for so long, as far back as I can remember, scared of the world and the people in it. Scared that the man I've fallen in love with would one day break my heart if I confessed my feelings to him. Not anymore. He's not just my alpha, not just the powerful man my biology chose as a mate based on primitive instincts alone. He's the one who sacrificed all to save me —he's the only one who will never, ever hurt me.

"I love you." I sob it out between gulps for air, my tears still flowing freely down my face. "I love you. I love you."

"Look at the TV."

I obey, sniffling and confused by his response to my declaration of love, but I obey.

Images of what looks like Mattenburg River by night taken from a helicopter capture my attention. A red banner across the top reads *"Breaking News."* There are flashing police lights down below, and when the camera zooms in, three body bags are clear on the river bank, circled in by police tape.

I blink and strain to hear what the commentators say over the rush of blood pulsing through my body.

"...bodies found only minutes ago. The police have confirmed that one of the drowned men is the former Lord Mayor Michael Bremen, who was dethroned last week by current Lord Mayor Peter Leod in a landslide election. No words yet on the identity of the two other men found in the river tonight, nor any official speculation on the cause of this incident. The Chief of Police has called for a press conference at eight o'clock in the morning. Until then, we can do nothing but mourn the passing of one of Mattenburg's most prominent figures."

"He took you from me." Peter's growl is deep and filled with emotion—with hate, and something else. Something vulnerable and soft that makes my heart flutter in my chest despite the knowledge of what he's done.

"He threatened to hurt you, and so he had to die. The two men they found with him are the ones who dared put their hands on you under his command."

"You killed them," I whisper, but the roil of emotion in my gut is not from horror. "If the police discover it was you—"

"They won't." He punctuates the short statement with a slow, agonizing movement forward of the fist lodged deep in my pussy. I cry out as tensed flesh tightens desperately around his thick fist, trying and failing to contain the motion. He slides his hand all the way up to let his knuckles brush gently over my cervix before he pulls back, the heel of his hand threatening to pop out of my straining sheath still clinging onto him for all its worth.

When he reverses the movement and pushes back in, my brain short circuits and my body takes over.

"And even if they did, I wouldn't let anyone tear us apart. Not now, not ever. You're the only one I will ever love, Leigh. The only one. If you demand it, I will conquer armies for your affection, and I will *kill* every man, woman, and child who dares lay a finger on you. My life, my power, is yours. As long as I breathe, I will be yours to command. Yours to love. *Yours.*"

For every sentence he pumps his fist into me, faster and faster, forcing obscene, wet slurps from my conquered pussy, and I howl in response, too lost in the brutal fisting to form words. There is nothing in my world but his fist and the slick, vanquished depths of my trembling sex, nothing but my own perfect surrender even as he promises me servitude.

When he rolls my clit between the fingers not buried to the forearm inside of me, it's like the last thread tying me to my own humanity snaps.

I roar like a wounded beast, my pussy clamping down so hard around his still-pumping arm that his bones groan in protest, and I *come*. I come, and he fists me through it while I thrash and scream and beg. And I come again, as my body shakes with pleasure so intense I plead for mercy. And again. And again.

He only stops fisting me when my legs give out and I slump over the backrest of the couch, so spent that the edges of my vision threaten my consciousness with plumes of black.

The room falls silent around us, save for the monotone chatter on the TV and our ragged gasps for air. He holds his fist still inside of me until my body finally stops trembling. And then, narrowing his hand as much as his bones will allow, he eases it out of my weeping pussy.

I whimper at the loss when he finally pulls free of my clinging flesh, and I am left gaping open and so empty I feel it all the way to my womb. Every nerve below my navel is throbbing with dulled sensation, making my swollen sex clench around air in search of the intimate connection I've lost.

But I am not empty for long.

The sound of a zipper being lowered is followed by hands against my sex, pulling my tender lips apart—and then an achingly familiar, hard heat presses against my opening and pushes inside with only my broken cry as resistance.

Peter sheathes his thick cock inside my swollen and overstimulated pussy in one long stroke. He doesn't give me time to adjust, only wraps his arms around my torso and lifts me up against his chest to support my body against his before he fucks me like the alpha he is.

His hoarse grunts of pleasure are punctuated by my whimpers every time he bottoms out in my depths. I'm too exhausted to even moan, but when he slides his right hand down my body to find my sore clit, I can't fight against the inevitable.

Despite every cell in my body screaming in protest, his rough strumming of the engorged nub of nerves paired with the unrelenting slide of his thick cock inside of my raw depths has the desired effect. When his knot finally catches inside the mouth of my pussy and his sperm spurts deep into my conquered sheath, I come for him one final time.

Just as I tumble over the cliff of madness with a sob, he clamps his teeth shut around the back of my neck and bites down until he breaks through my skin with a snarl. Marking me as his mate for the rest of time.

I fall into blessed unconsciousness with Leod's unbreakable promise of forever etched into my skin and singing through my soul.

EPILOGUE

3 MONTHS LATER

"And how is life as the Lord Mayor's mate?"

Three months after Peter bit my neck and branded my flesh with his claiming mark, I still don't know how to answer this question.

I smile politely at the reporter who has stuck her microphone in my face. She works for a rival network, but tonight my job isn't to ask questions. Tonight, on the Lord Mayor's arm, I'm here to answer them.

"Wonderful," I say, and it isn't a lie, but it isn't the whole truth either. "He has been so busy working for the city after the election, but he still manages to be the sweetest and most attentive mate a woman could hope for. I am truly blessed."

His PR team has crafted this answer. I approved it, of course, and it's with some relief I repeat it to the curious public, who are endlessly interested in how their favorite politician acts at home. Not that I can really blame them, after the eye-opening video of his more primal side they were all treated to. Were I to attempt a real explanation of the depth of emotion between us or the strength of our union, it would be far more intimate, far more violating than when the entire world watched us on said video.

The truth is that someone who hasn't experienced a mate claim will never be able to understand what it's like, no matter the intrusiveness of their questions.

"So no regrets?" the reporter asks.

"No. Never." I shake my head, and regret the motion when the nausea that's been plaguing me for the past few weeks rears up, this time joined by a dizzy spell. I stumble a step down the stairs in my high heels, but the reporter catches me by the elbow before I can go ass over teakettle.

"Oops! Are you alright, Mrs. Leod?" she asks, a flare of genuine concern flickering in her eyes.

Mrs. Leod. Even now hearing my new title makes warmth bubble within me. We didn't have a grand wedding; when Peter claimed me, we were officially wed in the eyes of the law, and after our relationship was publicly revealed, we both wanted to keep this one thing just for us.

Naturally there was an announcement from Town Hall and a mob of photographers eternalizing the fresh scar on my neck across the city's front pages, but no poufy dress, no speeches, and no public explanation for why the Lord Mayor's bride didn't have any family show up for her big day.

I offer the reporter a softer smile in return as I right myself. "Yes, thank you. Just lost my step—"

I'm going to say more—place the blame on my high heels and the long evening—but I don't get the chance. Peter puts his hand on my shoulder, steadying me as he turns me halfway around.

"You okay?" His voice is gruff, his eyes flickering over my face and down my body in search of injuries before they lock on mine. Worry flares in them, and I give him a grin.

"Yeah, I'm good. Just a bit of a wobble. High heels, you know? Weren't you in the middle of having your picture taken with some fancy CEO, Lord Mayor?" I tease, turning to the reporter, who's clearly delighted at witnessing Peter's work façade dropping in favor of his role as an alpha concerned for his mate. "I told you he's very attentive."

The woman giggles a bit and shifts the microphone to Peter. "How is mated life treating you, Lord Mayor? Some would say it's a big responsibility to take on so soon after assuming the mantle of running Mattenburg."

"*Some*" being his opponents attempting to sow concern about Peter's ability to lead when his focus is likely on his new mate.

"Leigh is my soul," Peter says, his gaze remaining on mine for a second longer before he turns to the reporter—to his job. "And these past months, we have all seen how determined she is to bring a brighter tomorrow to Mattenburg. She would murder me if I so much as thought about stepping down. A commitment to her is a commitment to our city."

"Aww," the reporter coos. "You two really are the perfect couple."

It's hard to argue with that when Peter smiles politely before wrapping his arm around my back, taking most of my weight as he excuses us and starts guiding me toward the car at the bottom of the steps. He can feel my exhaustion in our bond, and I feel his concern in return. We are in the backseat, and the driver is pulling away from the throng of reporters when he voices it.

"What's wrong, Leigh?"

I give him a tired smile and push off my heels to stretch my toes with a hum of relief. "Nothing, baby. I'm just exhausted. It's been a busy few weeks, and tonight was a long night. The glitz and glamour of mayoral prominence is all well and good, but some of us prefer to be in bed before midnight."

He grunts and grabs for my leg. I obediently swivel around in my seat to lean against the car door so I can place my feet in his lap.

"And the doctor didn't find anything?" he asks—for the twentieth time in the past three days since he forced me to see a physician.

"No," I sigh, giving him an eyeroll for good measure.

"I'll arrange for another doctor to see you for a second opinion," he says, absentmindedly pushing his thumb into the arch of my foot.

I swallow a moan of pleasure and give him a stern

look. "You're being overbearing. I'm fine, love. I promise. I'm just tired."

He frowns deeper. "You nearly fainted tonight. I felt you. If you're this exhausted, we need to cut your hours. Your editor is demanding too much of you. And so is Norman."

"No." I pull my foot out of his grasp and give him a light kick to get him out of this particular spiral. *"We* are not cutting my hours. *I* decide if and when I want to pull back, not you, bossy pants. If you want to help me get more sleep, you can always decide to cut out the nightly sex marathons. That's three hours of extra sleep I could be having."

Peter glances to the front of the car, where the driver is very determinedly not smirking in the rearview mirror. Narrowing his eyes, my mate pushes the button to roll up the separation, offering us some privacy before he returns his focus to me.

"Leigh—"

"Peter," I interrupt him. "I understand that you're concerned, and I love you for caring. But you need to listen when I tell you I'm fine. And you don't get to call the shots when it comes to my employment."

He stares at me for a long time, and I see the darkness he's fighting. Finally he heaves a deep sigh and pulls my foot back to rub at it. "Fine. I won't have your hours cut. But you need to see another doctor. That's non-negotiable."

I arch an eyebrow at him, even as he pulls a moan of

pleasure from me with those skilled hands of his. "Non-negotiable?"

"Yes. Non-negotiable."

I SWING my feet as I sit on the examination table, waiting for the doctor to see me. Turns out Peter wasn't kidding about the non-negotiable part. He was, in fact, serious enough that he's forced some poor physician to work a Saturday morning just for me.

In the grand scheme of things, it's fine. I know my mate struggles with his alpha instincts. I know he's trying his best not to smother me with his desperate urge to keep me safe. Every morning I get ready to leave for my day job is a fight for him, and I know the command that I stay by his side is just on the tip of his tongue. Yet he never voices it—even if no other reporter in history has gone to work with as big a security detail as I constantly have on my ass.

Insisting he gets to make sure I don't keel over and die on him? All right. I'll take it.

The door to the brightly lit examination room swings open and a man wearing a white lab coat enters. He's looking at a clipboard, and from the mussed state of his hair and slightly pink tone to his eyes, I'm guessing he was out celebrating having the weekend off.

"Sorry. I tried telling him to at least wait until Monday," I say.

The doctor looks up from his clipboard and offers me a smile. "It's fine. The Lord Mayor is not the first newly mated alpha to call me at five a.m. on a Saturday. Now what can I do for you, Mrs. Leod? Your mate says you've been struggling with exhaustion to the point of nearly passing out? And that you have a hard time keeping food down?"

I roll my eyes. "He's dramatic that way. I just had a little stumble. There's nothing wrong with me. I'm pregnant."

Saying it out loud gives the same kind of sucking feeling low in my gut as when the first doctor told me the news.

"Oh! Congratulations!" The doctor's smile widens. "No wonder your mate is a bit, ah, overprotective. Alphas usually make intensely overbearing first-time fathers."

I grimace. "I haven't told him yet."

The doctor's smile turns into a small frown. "Oh?"

"He's got a lot on his plate. I don't know how he's going to handle *this* on top of everything else." I gesture to my abdomen. "We haven't really had time to have *the talk*. I'm not even sure if he *wants* kids, let alone in his first year as mayor."

There is kindness is the doctor's eyes when he puts a hand on my wrist. "And you, Mrs. Leod? Do *you* want a child now?"

I bite my lip. In the turmoil of thoughts that have been warring in my mind since I first found out, that question somehow never popped up. I've worried if Peter wants a child now, if his opponents will use it against him, and... in the most private of moments, I've worried if this will be what finally snaps his resolve to allow me my freedom. If knowing I carry his baby will taint his protectiveness with the darker aspects of his nature.

But I've never questioned my own desire to become a mother. Because...

I nod, looking down to hide the tears stinging my eyes. "Yeah. I do."

Before Peter, I was alone for a long time. I'd chosen to focus on my career and my career alone because the yawning chasm of loneliness pulling on me was too scary to face. But in the most private parts of my heart, I've always longed for this: a family of my own.

He's given me everything, my alpha—his love, his protection, career advancement—everything I've ever wished for and more. Including *a child*.

Gentle fingers wipe away the tears dripping onto my cheeks. I look up at the doctor, who's smiling at me. "Then let's get you checked out so we can make sure that both you and your baby are in tip-top shape, hmm? And when you're ready to tell him, I am certain the Lord Mayor will be nothing but thrilled with the news."

THE DOCTOR SENDS me home with a stack of prenatal vitamins and orders to cut down on my workload so I can rest.

Prescribed naps. Not the worst outcome of a doctor's appointment.

The bond tying me to my mate hums with increasing agitation in my chest, and I rub at my ribs and fish my phone out to see what's up. Our connection always lets me know with all possible clarity when my alpha's waiting for me to respond.

And yup, Peter's called me five—yes, *five*—times during my appointment, and left three voicemails and seven texts demanding I tell him if anything's wrong.

I grimace, but can't help but crack a smile as I type out a text assuring him I'm not about to die. He is so not a patient man.

- What is it, then?

His response is immediate, and I hesitate with my thumbs hovering over my phone's display. I don't think I'm ready to tell him yet. I need—

My phone jumps to life with a persistent buzzing in my hand. Peter's name flashes, and I answer more out of habit than any desire to deal with my agitated mate over the phone.

"*Leigh. What is it?*" are his first words.

"Jesus, you really need to learn some chill. It's just exhaustion—like I told you," I say. It's an easy lie, but I still feel guilty.

A small pause. *"Alright, I'll finish up and come home. These reports can wait until Monday."*

I smile despite myself. I might call it overprotectiveness and roll my eyes at him, but deep down it feels pretty good that he cares so much for my wellbeing.

"You don't need to do that. I'm just gonna get some lunch and crawl into bed. I'm fine, baby. Don't stress about me, okay?"

He chuffs through his nose. We both know he's physically incapable of relaxing when it comes to me.

"I'll be home when you get there," he says, a note of finality to his voice I've come to know all too well these past few months. *"Stay safe."*

I sigh, knowing that this particular hill isn't worth dying in. "Okay. You too. Love you."

"I love you too, mate," he says before the connection dies.

I cling those words as I get into the car waiting to take me home. He loves me—enough that he's fought his urge to dominate and possess me like his father did with his mother. Hopefully that will still be the case once I tell him.

I WALK in the door to our penthouse apartment and am immediately greeted by strong arms wrapping around my body.

"Hey," I say into Peter's thickly muscled chest, my

greeting somewhat muffled by his shirt as he hugs me tightly.

"Hey," he murmurs, bending to push his nose into my neck so he can inhale my scent. It's his usual greeting—he's explained it soothes his more primitive instincts to smell me after being separated. I just think it's kinda cute.

"Did you get hassled for leaving early?" I ask, pulling back to look up at him.

"Of course. Norman doesn't give a shit about weekends. I swear that man needs to get a girlfriend before he drives someone to commit murder." His eyes scan my face. "You look pale."

"I'm tired," I say with a smile meant to comfort him. I can feel his unease in our bond and put a hand to his chest where his end is hooked. "Please don't worry about me, Peter. It'll make me worry about *you*."

He returns my smile, a slightly forlorn look on his handsome features. "You may as well ask me to stop breathing."

"That would be very impractical. And it would do nothing to stop me worrying," I tease.

Peter chuckles and scoops me up into his arms, bridal-style, before placing a kiss on the top of my head. "Indeed. So don't ask me to do what you know to be impossible. Now come—let's have lunch."

I hum happily and relax in his arms as he carries me into the living room and deposits me on the sofa. A large tray of sushi is laid out on the coffee table.

"What's that? Did the doctor give you medicine?"

Peter draws my attention from the raw fish to the white paper bag still dangling from my hand—the paper bag containing my prenatals.

"Oh, um, no, just some vitamins," I say, moving my hand and bag away as he goes to grab it from me.

Peter narrows his eyes at me. "Leigh... What are you hiding?"

"I'm not—"

"Don't lie to me." His voice isn't angry or threatening. It's quiet—soft. Vulnerable.

I look back at the sushi and bite my lip.

"Please, mate," he whispers, "whatever it is, just tell me."

He's so scared. I feel his rising panic in our bond, and my guilt swells up like bile in my throat. I turn back toward him and reach for his hands.

He takes mine and sinks down on the sofa sideways so we are face to face. In his eyes I see the naked fear that's currently making our bond hum out of tune—but also resolve. He's bracing for the worst possible outcome.

"I'm pregnant," I say.

For a long moment, he just stares at me.

"Please say something," I plead once the sound of our breathing becomes too much to bear.

"What?" His voice is hoarse—raw.

"I'm... I'm pregnant," I repeat. "About three weeks, the doctor estimated. He said it's not unusual for it to happen outside of heats, and we haven't exactly been careful. I know we should have probably talked about this, or like... used condoms. But... Peter, I want to keep it."

He blinks. "What do you mean—*keep* it? Of course we're keeping our baby, Leigh! What—What on Earth did you think I was going to suggest?"

He releases one of my hands to rub his scalp. The expression in his eyes is kind of wild. Shock slowly starts to overtake the panic I can feel from him.

"Pregnant?" he asks as if he suspects he's either heard wrong or I'm pranking him.

"Yeah." I give his hand a squeeze. "I know it's soon—"

"Pregnant," he interrupts me. And then, slowly, a smile spreads on his soft lips, the warmth of it penetrating through my flesh and into my heart, heating it in a way I didn't know was possible. "We're... We're having a baby?"

"Yes." Despite my worry, I can't help but return his smile as he gently places his hands over my abdomen.

For a long moment we sit in silence, both of us staring at his palms on my stomach.

"So... you're happy?" I finally ask.

He looks up at me then, and there's a light in his eyes that makes my heart flutter. Without a word he wraps his arms around me and pulls me out of my seat and into him. Kisses land on my hair, cheeks, forehead, nose, and finally my lips. Our bond *sings*.

Words are unnecessary, but after a long while, he finally pulls back and whispers, "Yes. Very, very happy, mate. I was hoping... But I didn't think it would happen until perhaps your next heat."

Wait. He was *planning* for this? I stare at him, dumbstruck. "Uh... you never said anything. Should you maybe have talked to me about this...?"

He blinks again, surprise on his face. "We're mated. Of course I want a child with you." Then something shifts in his beautiful eyes and he frowns.

"What?" I ask.

He gives me a long look, mouth pulling into a line even as he rubs his knuckles over my lower back. "Why were you trying to keep this a secret?"

"Oh." I bite my lip and lower my gaze. I don't want to hurt him, and the truth is going to hit him in one of his few vulnerable spots.

"Just tell me," he says, moving his hand from my back to my head to smooth my hair.

I draw in a big breath before forcing myself to look back up at him. "I am scared this will... make your instincts take over."

His frown deepens, and there is a dark shadow in his eyes, but he doesn't reply.

"Even the doctor said that alphas get overbearing when their mates are pregnant. I know how hard it already is for you to give me the freedom to go where I please, to work... I can feel your struggle here." I press my free hand to my ribs. "With a baby... I just... I'm not ready to give up my career, or my freedom."

He stares at me for a long time. Then he stands and offers me a hand. "Come."

I take it on instinct and he pulls me to my feet, only to scoop me into his arms once more.

"I can walk," I say as he carries me to the hallway. He's always had a penchant for carrying me around like I'm some delicate china doll. Sometimes it's sweet, sometimes it's sexy. Sometimes it's kinda annoying.

He only grunts in reply, opens our front door, and continues to the elevator.

"Where are we going?" I ask when he hits the button to the basement level where the parking garage is located. We usually don't go past the ground floor—Peter normally has his driver take us where we need to go—but I know he has a sporty Lexus stored down there.

"I'll explain when we get there," he says, and I resign myself to my fate. Our bond is humming with an odd energy and I don't want to push him. I hurt him by telling him why I'd been reluctant to share my pregnancy news, that much is obvious. Hurting Peter feels a bit like stabbing myself in the gut. *Damn bond.*

HE DRIVES us southeast out of the city until high-rises are replaced by cornfields. We're forty minutes down the highway before he turns off by a sign marked *RUTHVILLE – 3 MILES*.

It turns out to be a small, rural town. Rundown shops line the main street, and there's only a few people going about their business as we drive through. Peter stops by a gas station next to a feed store, pops in, and returns with a bouquet of somewhat wilted sunflowers. He tosses it onto the backseat before he pulls back out onto the road.

"Uh...?" I ask, eyeballing the bouquet. He's bought me flowers before. Lots of them. They're always lush and bountiful—and expensive.

He doesn't reply, and I sink back into the passenger seat with a sigh. Hopefully we'll arrive at wherever we're going soon, because this brooding silence is going to drive me crazy.

I have my answer shortly after when Peter pulls up next to a cemetery, puts the car in park, and turns off the engine.

"We're here," he says, his voice somehow gruff and soft at the same time.

"Okay..." I unbuckle my seatbelt and almost make it out the door before my mate materializes by my side, reaching for me.

I hold up a hand to stop his attempt at picking me up again. "I can walk," I insist when he gives me an unhappy look.

Peter narrows his eyes for a moment, looking very much like he's about to argue, but for once he doesn't.

We walk through the main gates and into the cemetery in silence, his arm around my waist and his pace measured for my shorter legs. Rows and rows of tombstones pass us until he finally stops.

I look at the grave we're facing. It's unremarkable—

identical to the rest of them, if perhaps a bit more unkempt than most.

That is, until I read the inscription.

Mary Leod
Thomas Leod
Bound by Love

THERE ARE NO BIRTH DATES, and no date of death either.

Peter bends to place the bouquet of sunflowers against the tombstone. He brushes a bit of dirt away from the engraved "M" with his thumb before he steps back.

"Your parents," I say softly, placing my hand on his arm. He doesn't come here often—not once while we've been together, and perhaps not for some time before that, judging from the look of the grave. He hasn't mentioned them much either.

"He brought her sunflowers. Every Sunday. It was the one thing that could make her smile. Sometimes," he says, and I realize that my flowers always arrive on Sundays too. My heart clenches.

"Peter," I whisper, and though I don't know what else to say, I know he feels my empathy in our bond.

He places his hand on top of mine and squeezes it. "He died within an hour of her. He held her hand until she expired, and then he simply... fell to the floor. Clutching his chest." Peter touches his own chest where our bond attaches on his end. "It's the only time I ever saw him cry. He wept and wept... and toward the end, he pleaded for absolution. Begged her to forgive him. I think when death finally took him, it was a mercy."

"You saw it?" I ask, horrified and aching for the pain he went through—the pain he still carries with him now.

He nods, never taking his eyes off the tombstone. "That's what will happen to me too. When you die."

"I mean, you could die before me," I say. It's meant as a lighthearted comment to ease the mood, but he only shakes his head.

"No. I will never put you through that kind of pain. *I* claimed you—that's my burden to bear. No matter what we'll face together, I will not die before you are ready to take your last breath, my mate. This I swear to you."

He finally turns around to face me, and in his eyes I see all the pain and grim determination—and a love so deep it still takes my breath away.

"Whenever I think of my parents, I think about that hour after my mother died. The anguish on my father's face, the regret. The knowledge that he and he alone took away everything that was beautiful and strong about her spirit.

"I know you feel my struggle—feel how much I yearn to keep you tied to my side night and day. To never let you out of my sight. But Leigh... just the thought of sitting by your side when you take your last breaths and knowing that I might have done anything to quell your light, your strength... it's unbearable.

"Throughout our short time together, I've learned... so much. About you, and about myself. I know I've not been good at putting it into words. Give me an audience in need of dazzling and I'll speak for hours, but *you*..." He gives me a small smile. "You make me feel like a tongue-tied adolescent. How can I explain to you how fundamentally you've changed my understanding of everything I once thought to be true? How just the thought of damaging your wild, beautiful spirit makes me sick?"

Peter breathes in deeply and reaches out to stroke a hand through my hair. "When our day comes I will sit by your side, I will hold your hand, and we will talk about all our beautiful memories, and the dark ones too, but there will be no regrets. So no, Leigh. Even our child won't make me lose control of my instincts. I am always going to protect you, and part of that is making sure you are happy. And free."

He turns his gaze back to the grave, eyes darkening. "I will never deprive our child of knowing you—the real you, not some shadow I've created. I promise you, mate."

I wipe at the tears stinging my eyes before stepping into him to rest my cheek against his chest. Peter enfolds me in his arms, an instinctive reaction to my closeness, followed by a kiss to the top of my head.

I stare at his parents' tombstone in silence while he holds me, my thoughts returning to the life I now carry. And for the first time, the thread of joy that's been trying to sprout ever since I first learned of my pregnancy breaks through the fear and uncertainty, welling up within me until all that's left is light and love and the deepest gratitude.

"We're going to have a baby," I whisper.

"Yes. We are," he says so softly it makes me shiver.

"Norman's gonna have a cow."

Peter chuckles. He lets one hand slip from my back around to my abdomen, cradling my nonexistent baby bump. "You say that, but he's been hounding me to knock you up ever since we made your claiming public. Something about voters loving a family man."

I snort. "Glad my uterus and I can be of service."

He hums and pulls his hand from my belly to nudge my chin up, catching my gaze with his. "I *am* going to be a family man, Leigh. You and our children will always come first. Mayoral title or no."

There is absolute sincerity in his eyes, and in the bond in my chest.

"I know," I tell him, because I do. There is no more doubt in my mind, and no more fear. This man has proven himself to me again and again, and now, here, by his parents' grave...

I turn my head back around to look at the tombstone.

Bound by Love.

I know why Peter chose that engraving. He did it out of anger and sorrow for what his parents' bond did to them. What it cost *him*.

Yet now he is no less bound by his own mating, only our love is anything but a burden.

"If you don't have any objections, I would like to name our daughter Mary. Or our son Thomas," I say.

He exhales above me and once more wraps me in his arms, nuzzling his face against the side of my neck where his mark lies.

"I would like that," he murmurs to me. "I would like that very much."

EZBAN CONFINEMENT FACILITY, LOCATION: CLASSIFIED

INMATE 50063

"The new batch has been prepped per your instructions, Doctor." That annoying, grating voice I've come to loathe floats through the bars and into my cell.

In my time on death row, I've known many guards, all of them cruel, but this man... This man makes my teeth hurt with an insurmountable ache to tear into his throat and rip until blood fills my mouth.

"Good. Any notes my staff should be aware of? We want our team to be safe." A new voice. Cold, condescending. And alpha.

My muscles tense as instincts roar to the surface. I thrash against the metal binds locking me in place to the gurney I've been strapped to for the past eight hours, battle lust throbbing in my blood.

"Yes. This one." Two sets of footsteps pause outside my cell, and I snarl a challenge out. They're watching me bound and helpless, and fury pounds in my temples as I fight the constrictions to free myself. Every cell in my body aches to maim, to *kill!*

"Inmate 50063. He's responding well to the drugs, but we haven't seen this level of rage in any of the other alphas we've prepped. We had to double his tranq dosage to prep him for transport. He maimed two of my coworkers yesterday. Sonuvabitch was vicious even before your drugs. Now, he's lethal."

"Hmm." Rustling of papers. "Let's see what we have here, then. Ex-navy. Tried for murder and treason? My, my. I'd like a closer look. Unlock the door—let's have a peek at this alpha."

"As you wish, Dr. Axell," the guard says. There's glee in his voice. He hopes this alpha doctor is going to hurt me.

I snarl another challenge. Let him try. I've endured everything a human can in this godforsaken place. Nothing he can do will break me.

Clanging of the keys is followed by the screech of the metal door swinging open. One set of footfalls enter my cell, stopping by my side.

I glare up at the stranger. He's definitely an alpha—his scent hits my nostrils and I growl at him, daring him to do his worst.

He only smiles mildly in response. "Look at you. What a prime specimen you are—big and strong and so fierce, hmm? You're not the least bit intimidated by me, even tied up and at my mercy, are you?"

"No." It's hard to form the word, my tongue fumbling to produce the sound.

The other alpha smiles wider. "Good. You'll need that fire. And so will we."

He flicks through the papers again, eyes scanning the pages. "I see you were deployed abroad during the uprising in Mattenburg and the subsequent power change in the city last year. Did you hear about it? Maybe watch that delicious sex tape of the new mayor?"

I glare at him. Everyone's watched that tape, even if my memory of it is fussy. Everything's fussy since they've begun injecting me daily. I try to force my brain into gear—the way this alpha is smirking, something about it is important. I need to understand... I growl, frustrated that my mind scatters and all I can focus on is the throbbing in my blood to fight this enemy standing over me. I strain, willing my muscles to rip through the restraints. Once again, they refuse to budge.

The doctor chuckles at my futile struggle. "What you may have failed to realize while you were jerking your dick to that pretty girl's squealing, is what my team and I did during that whole malarkey: any alpha, no matter how feral, will come to heel if his mate's in danger."

"So?" I growl it out, confusion mixing with my anger. An alpha's mate is his biggest weakness—that isn't news.

"So," he says, his tone mocking. "I work for a corporation that's been focused on national defense. You were a soldier—I'm sure you're intimately aware of the shortcomings of our troops. We want you stronger, fiercer... easier to control. By now you've likely noticed how your thoughts seems slower, hmm? How your temper's on a hair-trigger? How it's becoming difficult to remember words?

"The guards have been injecting you with a nifty little serum I developed. It relieves you of your higher brain functions, shutting off unnecessary activity until all that's left is raw, unbridled fire. Until you're the perfect soldier."

For the first time, something other than anger rises in my gut.

Fear.

"*No!*"

"Yes." The other alpha smiles down at me. "You will serve your country once more, but this time, there'll be no disobedience, and certainly no more treason. You won't ever refuse an order again—because if you do, your mate will suffer."

Confusion returns. I have no mate. "*What?*"

Dr. Axell chuckles once more at my bewilderment, a sound that now grates on me as much as the guard's voice. "Yes, you can thank Lord Mayor Leod for this light-bulb moment. You see, we've had such trouble getting our new super soldiers to obey. Strength and fury? Easy. The more feral you become, the stronger your instincts and therefore body. However, obedience? Much, *much* harder to provoke. But, in the end, it was such a simple solution.

"Once the drugs have taken away the last of your humanity, we will present you with a woman in heat. And you will claim her, because she will be the only source of pleasure for the rest of your miserable existence. The only way to make the pain stop for just a moment is through taking a woman as your mate. And when you do... we *own* you."

It takes several moments for his words to sink in.

He pulls a needle from his pocket and flicks the syringe, eyes trained on it as he adjusts the dosage of the liquid inside. Waiting for me to grasp my fate.

My roar of fury when the truth finally reaches my brainstem echoes through my cell as he jabs the needle into my arm, pushing the plunger down in one swift movement.

The last thing I see as my vision blurs and consciousness fades is his cruel face.

"Welcome to SilverCorp, test subject 351."

FERAL
CONTINUE TEST SUBJECT 351'S STORY

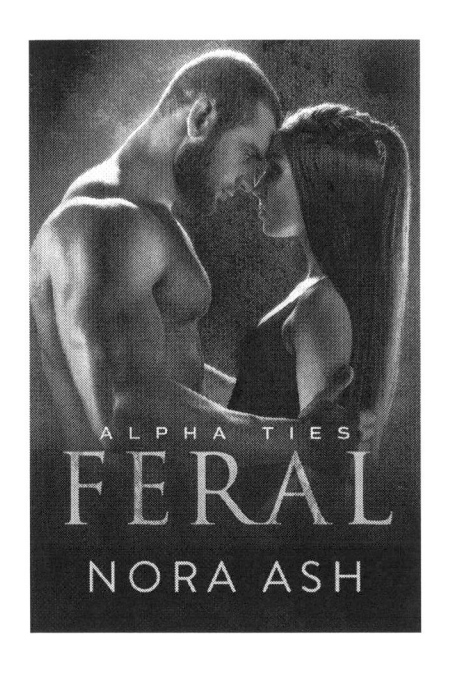

**I never wanted a mate.
But I was put in chains.
Strapped down.**

And claimed.

I always believed I could analyze any situation until I found a solution. Solve any problem if I just applied my brain.

I went to university, studied science and told myself my academic cocoon would protect me from the alphas dominating our society.

I was wrong.

NO TEXTBOOK PREPARED me for my meeting with test subject 351.

The biggest, scariest alpha on death row, hauled into my lab to uncover how to control the beast of a man. How to make him submit.

Mold him into a weapon.

But there is no controlling the feral alpha, and no logic strong enough to save my mind once he unleashes his fury on my body.

Once he claims me.

MORE FROM NORA

Join Nora's newsletter for updates on new books and free stories!

WWW.NORA-ASH.COM/NEWSLETTER

ALSO BY NORA ASH

FERAL SERIES
Obsession

Despair

Torment

THE OMEGA PROPHECY
Ragnarök Rising

Weaving Fate

DEMON'S MARK SERIES
Branded

Demon's Mark

Prince of Demons

DARKNESS SERIES
Into the Darkness

Hidden in Darkness

Shades of Darkness

Fires in the Darkness

ANCIENT BLOOD SERIES
Origin

Wicked Soul

Debt of Bones*

MADE & BROKEN SERIES

Dangerous

Monster

Trouble

Printed in Poland
by Amazon Fulfillment
Poland Sp. z o.o., Wrocław